Enjoy all of these American Girl Mysteries®:

THE SILENT STRANGER   A *Kaya* Mystery

LADY MARGARET'S GHOST   A *Felicity* Mystery

SECRETS IN THE HILLS   A *Josefina* Mystery

THE RUNAWAY FRIEND   A *Kirsten* Mystery

SHADOWS ON SOCIETY HILL   An *Addy* Mystery

THE CRY OF THE LOON   A *Samantha* Mystery

MISSING GRACE   A *Kit* Mystery

CLUES IN THE SHADOWS   A *Molly* Mystery

THE PUZZLE OF THE PAPER DAUGHTER   A *Julie* Mystery

and many more!

— A *Rebecca* MYSTERY —

SECRETS AT
CAMP NOKOMIS

by Jacqueline Dembar Greene

Questions or comments? Call 1-800-845-0005, visit our Web site
at **americangirl.com**, or write to Customer Service, American Girl,
8400 Fairway Place, Middleton, WI 53562-0497.

Printed in China
10 11 12 13 14 15 16 LEO 12 11 10 9 8 7 6 5 4 3 2 1

PICTURE CREDITS
The following individuals and organizations have generously given
permission to reprint illustrations contained in "Looking Back":
pp. 172–173—Courtesy of Camp Wohelo, www.wohelo.com (girls in tree house, canoes);
pp. 174–175—Library of Congress, Prints & Photographs Division, Detroit Publishing
Company Collection [LC-USZC4-1584] (Mulberry Street); © James Rudnick
(Grand Central Station); p. 176—Courtesy of Alford Lake Camp,
www.alfordlakecamp.com (campers in tent);
pp. 178–179—© Bettmann/Corbis (baby in window); March of Dimes Foundation (sign);
courtesy of the FDR library (braces); p. 180—courtesy of the FDR library
(President Roosevelt); March of Dimes Foundation (newspapers)

Illustrations by Jean-Paul Tibbles

Cataloging-in-Publication Data available from Library of Congress

*To my editor, Jennifer Hirsch,
and historian Mark Speltz,
with gratitude and friendship*

Table of Contents

1
ALL ABOARD

"Pay attention," Mama warned Rebecca. "I don't want to lose you in the crowd."

Rebecca could barely take her eyes from the brightly painted stars dancing across the dome of the train station. She had never imagined that Grand Central Terminal was so elegant.

Grandpa followed Rebecca's gaze. "In the country, you'll see real stars," he said, putting his arm around Rebecca's shoulder. "So close—you can almost touch them."

"You won't see stars if we don't find your camp group," Mama said. She craned her neck trying to see over the throngs of people. Families ushered children through the vast terminal, shouting over the echoing din of voices. Several men in sporty knickers stood near a marble

1

staircase holding camp banners. One read "Sunrise Lake Camp," and another "Camp Pinewood," but none named Rebecca's camp. Rebecca guessed that the young men must be counselors for boys' camps.

"There!" Mama announced, pointing to a tall woman in a yellow skirt holding a sign for Camp Nokomis. Rebecca's pulse raced. She was going to spend eight whole days in the countryside! If only her friend Rose were here, too. It would have been so much more exciting to be heading to camp together, as they had planned.

"It is good you can leave the city," Grandpa said. "You get fresh air, and even swimming, instead of heat and sickness all around."

Rebecca bit her lip at the mention of sickness. Grandpa didn't have to remind her that polio, a sudden illness that left many of its victims paralyzed, had begun to plague New York City. It seemed to strike children most. That's why Rose was at home while Rebecca was ready to board a train.

She and Rose had been thrilled when their

2

applications were chosen for the very first camp session. Every neighborhood family without money to spare signed their daughters up for the free camp. There were never enough spaces for everyone, but Rebecca and Rose had been among the lucky girls picked by the City Children's Society to attend Camp Nokomis.

Then, just a few days ago, a boy in Rose's building became ill with polio. City health workers nailed a quarantine sign on the front door. No one could go in or out of the building, in order to prevent the dangerous disease from spreading. Now poor Rose was stuck in her apartment, and Rebecca would be at camp without her.

"I wish I knew someone else going to Camp Nokomis," Rebecca said anxiously.

"You'll make new friends," Mama reassured her. Rebecca hoped Mama was right.

They pressed forward until they stood in front of the lady holding the camp sign.

"Your name?" the woman asked, looking down at Rebecca.

"Rebecca Rubin, Miss," she answered politely.

"I'm Miss Henry," the woman said, "and I'll be accompanying you on the train." She looked at Mama. "I'll need Rebecca's health certificate."

Mama handed Miss Henry the doctor's form that had been issued after Rebecca's physical exam. Miss Henry added it to a large envelope and checked off Rebecca's name on a neatly typed list. Rebecca saw some names with lines drawn through them and felt a pang of sadness. Maybe one of them was the name of her friend, Rose Krensky.

When all the girls were assembled, Miss Henry addressed the parents fussing over their daughters. "Don't worry a bit. The girls will be well cared for." Some parents had tears in their eyes as they hugged their daughters good-bye.

Mama kissed Rebecca on the cheek. "Do take care, Beckie," she said. She smiled, but Rebecca saw that her mother's eyes were moist. Rebecca felt a nervous flutter in her stomach. She truly wanted to go to camp, but without Rose, it was harder to leave.

4

With Miss Henry leading the way, the girls trooped off, clutching carpetbags and cardboard suitcases. They gawked at the huge glass windows in the station and the seemingly endless stairway. As they neared the tracks, the sound of chugging train engines filled the terminal.

"Here's our train car, girls," Miss Henry announced. "All aboard!"

Miss Henry carefully counted heads as the girls found seats in a passenger car. Rebecca slid into a window seat. In moments, the train blasted a piercing whistle and clattered out of the station. Rebecca felt her stomach lurch. She really was going away to the country—all by herself.

Miss Henry raised her voice above the noisy train wheels as they clacked along the iron tracks. "This is the smallest group we've ever had," she said, frowning at her list. "Unfortunately, several campers canceled at the last moment, and it was too late to contact more girls." She pasted on a faint smile. "Aren't you lucky! You'll have lots of space inside your tents.

You'll learn to swim, and canoe, and make some lovely crafts. Not to mention there will be an abundance of nutritious food." Then she added with a grin, "And some not-so-nutritious toasted marshmallows!" A few girls clapped their hands in delight.

Swimming! Canoeing! Rebecca felt sorry for anyone who had to miss such a wonderful trip. Perhaps, like Rose, some girls were stuck in quarantined tenements—or worse, maybe they were sick themselves. Rebecca tried not to think too much about Rose.

She glanced at the other girls, wondering if they wanted new friends, too. Some of them already knew one another. They hugged and laughed and chattered about all they had done in the past year. They barely looked at the new campers.

Rebecca turned to the girl sitting next to her. "I'm so excited," she said brightly. "Aren't you?" But the girl just stared down at her lap. She was younger than Rebecca and seemed about to cry. Rebecca patted the girl's hand. "Don't worry, we're going to have a grand adventure," she said firmly. She tried to swallow the lump in her own throat.

Rebecca watched through the train window as city buildings flew by in a blur. Before long, the view changed to villages, trees, and fields. The train stopped at a few depots, and groups of boys poured out of the cars, ready to head to their camps. They shouted and jostled each other while chaperones herded them together. At last the train pulled into a small station, and Miss Henry clapped her hands for attention.

"Camp Nokomis girls, gather your belongings and file out in a ladylike manner, please." While the girls stood on the platform, Miss Henry dashed back into the train car to be certain no one had been left behind. Just in time, she stepped down as the whistle blew and the train pulled out of the station.

A sour-faced man in a stiff-collared shirt approached Miss Henry. "Jeremiah Turnbull," he said, extending his hand, "Chairman of the town health committee." Miss Henry introduced herself and stepped away from the girls. The two spoke quietly together and Miss Henry handed over the envelope containing the health certificates. The official riffled through them briefly before tucking the envelope under his arm and striding off.

A few townspeople milled around the station, but none smiled at the girls. Rebecca was relieved when a group of cheerful young women decked out in camp clothes approached.

"Welcome, campers!" one said.

A stout woman standing near the ticket window exclaimed, "Look at that!"

"Simply scandalous," sniffed her companion.

"Folks here don't think girls ought to be tramping around in bloomers," the counselor told the girls. "But what else would we tramp around in?" She did a couple of energetic jumping jacks.

Rebecca didn't care what the townspeople thought. She couldn't wait to change from her everyday dress and shoes into her new camp clothes. The City Children's Society had given the campers puffy bloomers and middy blouses with crisp sailor collars and blue bows. There were spiffy white sneakers and stockings, too. But Rebecca's most treasured item was a bathing dress. At last, she would learn to swim.

As Miss Henry rejoined the group, one of the counselors shouted, "We're off!" The girls formed a line behind her. Some of the counselors carried the bags that weighed down the youngest girls. They strode along the rough path with ease in their loose bloomers, while Miss Henry wobbled in her high button boots, her wide-brimmed hat bobbing and her skirt swishing.

Looking around, Rebecca saw colorful wildflowers blooming in green meadows. Above her, birds chirped and trilled in a cheerful chorus that filled Rebecca with a warm glow. She had never heard anything like it in the city.

"Look," shouted a camper, "strawberries!" They all turned their heads toward a field of low plants with bright red berries clustered under the leaves.

"Oh, I *adore* strawberries," gushed one of the girls.

"Maybe our cook will bake us strawberry pies," said a counselor.

"Humph," grumbled a redheaded camper. "There weren't any pies last year. The cook thought we should all eat an extra serving of broccoli for dessert, she did!" The redhead spoke with an Irish brogue, and Rebecca liked the lilting sound.

"Oh, Red, it wasn't that bad," another girl responded. "I think I remember you having a pretty healthy appetite." The redhead tossed her curly hair and ignored the comment.

"We were quite fortunate to hire a wonderful new cook this summer," said Miss Henry. "She's called Miss Pepper." The girls twittered at the cook's funny name.

"I hope she doesn't put pepper in our food!" one of the girls joked.

The path meandered through towering trees, and Rebecca sniffed the piney air. A soft bed of pine needles cushioned her feet. The forest grew deeper, and a thick canopy of leaves shrouded the sunlight. After a long walk through the woods, the girls passed under an archway. Overhead, a carved wooden sign read "Camp Nokomis."

Rebecca's breath caught in her throat. She had left the city behind as surely as if she had walked into another world. Instead of crowded apartment buildings and alleyways, the girls filed past a row of tents and entered a clearing. A towering wooden pole stood in the center with a flag waving in the breeze. Nearby, a dazzling blue pond glistened in the sunshine.

"I wish you all an enjoyable and productive stay," Miss Henry said. "I shall see you again in eight days." She walked toward a rough log building with an open porch.

A counselor stepped forward. She wore her hair in one long braid. "I'm Barbara," she said, "but everyone here calls me Babs. We'll be spending lots of time together in Crafts." Babs pointed away from the clearing to the row of tents. "You'll be assigned to a tent according to your age. The first tent is called Turtle, and it's for the eight-year-olds. Nine-year-olds are in Crane, and going up in age we have Deer, Beaver, and Loon." Rebecca counted on her fingers. She would be in Beaver.

The campers stared solemnly at Babs. "Don't look so serious," she said. "You're going to have a whopping good time!"

As the counselors introduced themselves and assembled their charges, Rebecca gazed at the pond. She could hardly wait to jump into the rippling blue water. Her eyes scanned the shoreline, where she saw a row of green, red, and yellow wooden canoes just waiting to slide across the gentle waves.

"Camp is so much better than being stuck at home," Rebecca said to an older girl standing next to her. The girl nodded and grinned. Rebecca couldn't wait for all the camp adventures to begin.

A slim, wavy-haired counselor called out in a perky voice, "Eleven-year-olds follow me to Beaver."

That's me! Rebecca realized and stepped forward. She thought the dimple-cheeked young woman looked sweet.

"I'm Virginia," said the counselor with a bright smile. "I'm so glad to meet you all."

Rebecca eagerly joined several girls as they approached the large white canvas tent. From the Loon tent next door came a rousing cheer. "Loonies, Loonies, hip, hip, hooray!"

The redheaded girl from the walk to camp was in Rebecca's group. She nodded knowingly. "Some of us have been here before," she said.

What fun, Rebecca thought. *I hope I'll be back next summer, too.*

The Beavers filed into the tent, and Rebecca looked around at the empty bunk beds and rough wooden floor. She was surprised to see a camper already making up a bottom bunk. She didn't recognize her from the train or the hike to camp. Of course, there were so many new faces, she easily could have missed her.

Virginia handed out bundles of sheets and striped wool blankets. "Can you make up your beds?" A few girls admitted they had never done it before. "Time to learn!" Virginia said. "I'll turn you into experts." As the girls collected their bedding, she told them, "There aren't many rules here, but making your bed each morning is one of them. I want to see tight corners! In addition, you'll be assigned a daily chore that must be done promptly and well. Never leave the campground without permission, and once you're in bed for the night, no wandering outside the tent. There are plenty of skunks, and last year campers saw a bear prowling around."

Rebecca gulped. Skunks and bears? The forest didn't seem as safe as her own street back in the city.

"Now, pick a bed and I'll give you a bed-making lesson," said Virginia. The girls looked at the two rows of metal bunks, uncertain which beds to choose.

The red-haired camper with the brogue took command. "I was here last year, so I'll help everyone set up," she said, turning to the girl closest to her. "You'll be up top here." Then she patted her hand on the lower bunk and turned to a second girl. "You take the bottom."

Rebecca could barely take her eyes from the girl's flaming copper-red hair. Her skin was as pale as Mama's milk pudding, and there was a sprinkling of cinnamon freckles across her nose and cheeks. Rebecca couldn't help but admire the confident way the girl went about organizing everyone. Although she still missed Rose, Rebecca suddenly felt certain she would make lots of interesting friends at camp, starting with the spunky redhead.

She assigned Rebecca to the bunk above the girl who had arrived first. The girl smiled and Rebecca beamed at her. She was sure they were going to become best friends.

The red-haired camper plunked her bedding on the bottom of one of the remaining empty bunks and set her carpetbag on the upper bed. "I guess I have this entire bunk all to myself," she announced. She sounded surprised, but Rebecca couldn't help wondering whether she had planned it that way.

Rebecca looked for a place to store her carpetbag and saw a flat-topped leather trunk near her bunk. "Is this where we put our things?" she asked her bunk mate.

"Oh, no," the girl said. "That's mine."

Rebecca stared at the large trunk. "How in the world did you carry it all the way from the train station?" she asked, setting her bag on a bench at the foot of the bunk bed.

"My mother had it sent," the girl responded.

Rebecca flapped open her bottom sheet and tried to reach up to make her bed. The girl below scooted out. "You can stand on the edge of my bed," she offered. She was dressed in a long, oversized jumper that nearly covered her feet. Rebecca tried not to stare at the ill-fitting dress.

"I'm Rebecca Rubin," she said. "What's your name?"

"Christina," the girl said in a soft voice. "Christina Pfeffer."

"Now that we're bunk mates," Rebecca said,

"we'll get to know each other really well." Stepping carefully onto the edge of Christina's bed, she tucked the bottom sheet tightly around the edges. Christina handed her the top sheet and then the blanket. The girl's wrists were as thin as straws, and bangs nearly hid her eyes.

"I can't wait to get out of this dress and put on my bloomers," Rebecca announced when her bed was made. There was a chorus of agreement from the other girls. They pulled bloomers and blouses from their bags. Christina untied a thick piece of twine that fastened the latch on her trunk. She opened the lid a crack, reached her hand inside, and pulled out her camp clothes.

The red-haired camper glared at her. "Hey, you're in the wrong tent. Beaver is for eleven-year-olds." She put her hands on her hips. "Sure an' you look like you belong with the Turtles!" The other girls chuckled, a bit nervously. Christina didn't reply but started to leave the tent, holding her clothes.

"Wait, where are you going?" Rebecca asked.

"The privy," Christina answered quietly. She

17

clumped down the steps, her hand sliding down the railing.

While the girls changed and put away their city clothes, Virginia checked each bed, helping to smooth and tighten covers and demonstrating the technique. Rebecca glanced up when Christina returned wearing long, baggy bloomers that reached well below her knees. Her stockings sagged against her thin legs. She was so small, Rebecca reflected, that all her clothes were probably too long for her.

Virginia called the girls together. "Let's get acquainted. We'll become friends a lot quicker once we learn each other's names."

The red-haired camper started off. "I'm Mary Margaret Bridget McBride," she announced. Christina was next and gave her name timidly.

"Christina?" Mary Margaret Bridget repeated. "We'll call you Teeny Tina!" Christina opened her mouth in a wide O, as if to protest, and then clamped it shut without a word.

"Nicknames are fine," Virginia said, "but everyone should be pleased with what she's called. Perhaps Christina wouldn't mind if we shortened her name to Tina."

All eyes turned to the girl, and she nodded faintly. The girls completed their introductions, and Rebecca tried to remember each name.

"You know," said Virginia, "the animal names for each tent are taken from the names of real Indian clans. The people in a clan were just like family, even if they weren't related." She smiled warmly at the girls. "Your tent mates in Beaver will be like a family, too."

Rebecca was delighted. This was exactly what she had hoped for—new friends who would be as close to her as sisters.

Mary Margaret Bridget tossed her curly red hair. "Let's all have similar nicknames to make Beavers special." She thought a moment. "I've got it. We'll pick names with matching endings!"

"Oh, that would be cute," another camper agreed.

Mary Margaret Bridget pointed to each girl in turn, dishing out nicknames lickety-split, as confidently as she had assigned each girl to a bunk. "Rebecca, you're Beckie," she announced, and Rebecca nodded. Her family often called her Beckie. Mary Margaret Bridget kept going. "Sonia, you can be called Sunny. Camilla, you're Cammie. Josephine—Josie! Roberta, you're a bit harder. How about Bertie? And Dorothea, you can be Dottie." She laughed and added, "Just don't act dotty!"

Rebecca was amazed that Mary Margaret Bridget had remembered every girl's name. She noticed that she had skipped Tina, though. Rebecca glanced at the redhead's mischievous green eyes and could tell that she wasn't going to stop calling Christina "Teeny," at least when Virginia wasn't around.

"What about you?" Bertie asked. "Are you just Mary?"

"She can't be just Mary," said Cammie. "She's a Beaver, so she needs a nickname that matches ours."

"How'd you get so many names, anyway?" Sunny asked.

"My mother says I'm named for a long line

of sainted women from County Cork." Mary Margaret Bridget tilted her chin up proudly. "Just don't you dare call me Red, like they did last year!"

"How about Rusty?" Josie suggested.

The girl made a sour face. "That's just as bad."

"I've got it," Rebecca said. "Since your names all come from County Cork, we'll call you Corky."

The girl's green eyes sparkled and she smiled at Rebecca. Then she turned to Virginia. "As for you, how about if we call you Ginny?"

The counselor laughed. "Why not? That's what my brothers call me."

Rebecca thought Corky had picked nifty nicknames. Everything at camp was relaxed, and now their names were, too.

"I'm going to let you get settled," Ginny said, "and check back in a little while." She pointed to a tent near the main lodge. "I share that tent with a few other counselors, so you can find me there if you need me."

As soon as Ginny was out of earshot, Corky

sidled up to Tina and said, "See? You have to be called Teeny or your name won't fit in with the rest of the Beavers." Tina frowned and turned away.

If we're to become fast friends, thought Rebecca, *this isn't a very good way to start.*

2
WINDIGOS IN THE WOODS

Rebecca finished her last mouthful of fried chicken and stared at her empty plate. "I can't believe how hungry I was," she said.

"You weren't alone. I've never seen so much food disappear so quickly," Ginny marveled.

The dining room was just through a door off the covered porch on the main building. Inside, a long table served as a buffet, and on the back wall there was a massive stone fireplace. Maybe they would roast marshmallows there!

Noisy chatter filled the hall until the camp director clinked his spoon against a glass. The room fell silent. "Welcome to Camp Nokomis," said the slightly built man, pushing his wire-rimmed glasses higher on his nose. The spectacles magnified the director's eyes, and with his large ears, Rebecca thought he resembled a rabbit. All he needed were whiskers.

"I'm Mr. DeAngelis," he said, "but you may call me Mr. Dee. There are just a few people you haven't already met. First, our camp nurse, Miss Jane." A plump, gray-haired woman stood and gave a friendly wave to the girls.

The campers at the Loon table clapped their hand in rhythm and chanted, "Nurse Jane, Nurse Jane, she will take away your pain!" Other tables picked up the chant until Mr. Dee tapped his glass once again with an insistent tinkling.

"Our waterfront director, Roger."

Again the Loon girls started up a refrain. "Roger, Roger, loves the Dodgers." A strapping young man stood up and pretended to swing a bat, and then put his hand above his eyes as if watching a ball hit out of sight. The girls cheered. "Home run!" they yelled.

"Just wait till you hear Roger's campfire stories," Ginny whispered. "They'll make your hair stand on end!" A ripple of excitement spread around the table.

"And now, the most important person here," said Mr. Dee, "our cook, Miss Pepper."

A short, reed-thin woman, no taller than Rebecca, stepped through the swinging kitchen door. She put up her hand for silence as the campers applauded. "I shall be preparing nutritious food each day and you may eat your fill. However, I don't want anything wasted, so I expect clean plates. You'll all return home healthier than when you arrived." She paused and surveyed the campers before her. "You'll be assigned chores to help clear the tables and keep the dining hall tidy. I have just one rule that is never to be broken—no campers in the dining hall between meals. No excuses!" Miss Pepper then turned on her heel and disappeared back into the kitchen. The door flapped open and closed behind her.

Mr. Dee cleared his throat. "Miss Pepper is going to prepare the best meals you've ever eaten, so let's all keep her happy." Rebecca thought that sounded like the toughest chore of all.

The girls cleared their plates, scraped the garbage into a metal pail, and slid the dishes into metal pans filled with hot soapy water. They wiped the tables clean and swept the floor.

The sun dropped lower in the sky as everyone gathered in the clearing, sitting on flat planks arranged around a ring of stones. In the center, wood was neatly stacked for a campfire. As dusk fell, Roger strode into the fire circle holding a flaming torch. He held it against the twigs stacked under the logs. Slowly the fire took hold and grew into a flickering blaze. Rebecca leaned toward the circle of light as Mr. Dee addressed the campers.

"The moon is nearly full," he said, pointing to the sky. "The Indians who once lived here called this the Strawberry Moon."

Rebecca turned to Tina. "I guess that's why there are so many strawberries in the fields. I wonder if Miss Pepper will serve some."

"I'll ask her," Tina offered.

Rebecca pulled back. "Oh, I wouldn't dare! I don't think she wants any requests from us."

Mr. Dee made a wide arc with his arm. "The beautiful forest around us has been perfectly described by the poet Henry Wadsworth Longfellow: 'This is the forest primeval, the murmuring pines and the hemlocks.' While you're at camp, you are going to hear another wonderful poem by Longfellow telling the legend of Hiawatha. Some say Hiawatha was an Indian chief who united the warring tribes in peace. Others believe he was the great-grandson of the moon and had magical powers." Mr. Dee continued, "Before bed each night, your counselors will read some of the poem. Each tent will choose a passage and stage it on the last night of camp. One camper will narrate while the rest act it out in pantomime."

They were going to put on a show! Rebecca felt a tingle of excitement. There was nothing she loved more than acting. It seemed as if the fire glowed brighter as she imagined the performance. Why, camp was going to be even more wonderful than she had dreamed.

Roger stood up, firelight flickering across his

face. A hush fell as he began to speak. "Long ago, an evil creature stalked the Indians who roamed this land." He swept his arms toward the towering pine trees. "In these very woods, people told of a monster called the windigo. It lurked in the shadows, and if it saw a child wandering alone, it caught that straggler for dinner." He snatched at the air, as if closing his hand around something. Rebecca swallowed hard.

Roger continued his story. "Hiawatha's father, the West Wind, sent him to get rid of all the dangers on earth, so that humans would be safe. Said the wind to Hiawatha,

> *Cleanse the earth from all that harms it,*
> *Clear the fishing-grounds and rivers,*
> *Slay all monsters and magicians,*
> *All the windigos, the giants,*
> *All the serpents . . .*

The girls were absolutely silent. Rebecca imagined Hiawatha as a strong young man like Roger. She whispered to Tina, "I hope Hiawatha really did get rid of all the windigos. I don't want to meet any monsters in the woods. That would be a lot worse than a skunk!"

Lowering his voice, Roger added. "All that was ever found of the windigo's victims were tiny bones—picked clean as toothpicks!"

Rebecca felt thrilling shivers along her back, and the campers tittered in delicious fright. "Oh, Ginny, you were right. Roger really is a wonderful storyteller," Rebecca whispered. Ginny smiled knowingly.

Dottie wrung her hands together. "I'm getting goose bumps!"

"Indian children had a favorite game they played to practice escaping," Roger explained. "They formed a line and snaked through the woods holding on tightly to the person in front of them. One person played the windigo and tried to capture the last child in line. Now that it's properly dark and the moon is casting shadows . . . you form the line, and I'll be the windigo!" Roger jumped forward and made a ferocious face. "If I catch you, I'll eat you up!"

Shrieking and laughing, the girls rushed to form a line, each holding on tightly to the waist of the girl in front of her. The line snaked around the dying campfire, through the clearing, and between the murky trees. In no time at all, Roger pulled away the last girl in line and walked her over to the campfire to sit out the rest of the game. Then he ran to catch the last one in line again.

Tina hadn't joined in at all. Rebecca dashed back to the campfire. "Come on, Tina," she coaxed, pulling her up. "It's not so scary. It's great fun!"

"I'm not afraid," Tina said with a smile, "just tired. Anyway, I'm enjoying myself just watching you all run around." She motioned toward the line of laughing girls. "Go ahead, and if you get caught, we'll sit here together."

Rebecca looked back as she squeezed into the middle of the line. Tina looked content, but Rebecca wished her bunk mate had joined in. When the game ended, the girls gathered behind their counselors, who held oil lanterns to light the way back to the tents. The campers were still squealing over the excitement of the game, and no one wanted to be last. They crowded together, playfully pushing and shoving. Between the tall black pines, stars glittered overhead like tiny candles. *Grandpa was right*, thought Rebecca. *The stars look close enough to touch.*

The girls changed into their nightclothes and lined up for the privy. Tina carried her nightgown and returned holding her bloomers.

Rebecca chuckled. "I'll bet you don't have any brothers or sisters."

"How did you know, Beckie?" Tina asked her.

"Because you're so shy about changing. I have two sisters and two brothers, and my sisters and I share one tiny bedroom. There's no room for privacy!"

The girls slipped under the crisp sheets, and Ginny settled on a canvas stool. By the glow of the oil lamp, she read several pages from *The Song of Hiawatha.* When she finished, she told the girls that each night the campfire would end with the song "Taps." "I'll sing it for you tonight," she said, "and you'll learn it instantly." Her voice rose sweet and clear. "Day is done, Gone the sun, From the lake, from the hills, from the sky. All is well, safely rest, God is nigh."

"I'll be checking on you later tonight," Ginny said, "and expect you all to be sound asleep." She left quietly and dropped the tent flaps behind her.

"Say," Cammie whispered into the silence, "does anyone think there's really such a thing as a windigo?" She tried to sound unconcerned, but Rebecca heard a quiver in her voice.

"I don't know," replied Dottie, "but the windigo reminds me of the Russian witch Baba Yaga."

"Ooh, my grandmother told me about Baba Yaga," Sunny piped up. "She ate up children who happened upon her house in the forest."

"Don't be silly," Bertie argued. "They're all just made-up stories."

"My bubbie said Baba Yaga is real," Sunny insisted, "so maybe the windigo is, too."

"Want to know something I heard last year?" Corky asked.

"Tell us," the girls clamored.

"Well," Corky said, "last year I heard some counselors talking about the windigo. They didn't know I was listening, but I heard every word."

"What did they say?" the girls asked breathlessly. "Tell us!"

"They said—" Corky paused dramatically. "Well, they said there's a cave not far from here where the windigo *lives*." Gasps echoed through the tent. "When I heard that, I knew that was why they tell us never to go into the woods alone."

The girls fell silent. Rebecca imagined a monster lurking in a shadowy cave, just waiting for a camper to pass by. She lay awake listening to the unfamiliar sounds around her—a repeated chirp, a high-pitched hum, and a chorus of peeps from the pond. She tried not to let them

frighten her. She was used to city sounds—
people talking and laughing in the street below,
horse-drawn wagons clattering by at all hours,
trains rattling by, and ship horns across the
river. *Why, these are just normal country sounds,*
she told herself—*bugs and frogs.* Then an eerie
hooting echoed through the woods. *Ta-whoo!*
Ta-whoo! Rebecca's breath caught in her throat.

That was no frog! She thought of the strange
tale Roger had told of the windigo and remembered the Baba Yaga tales her grandmother had
told her when she was small enough to sit on
Bubbie's comfortable lap. What if scary stories
weren't made-up but told of things that truly
happened, as a warning? In spite of the warm
air, Rebecca drew the covers over her head and
pulled them tightly around her.

3
PRANKS AND CHORES

A tinny blast jolted Rebecca awake. The other girls groaned as the bright notes were repeated.

"That's the bugle playing 'Reveille,'" Corky announced. "Rise and shine, lassies!"

"I saw a bugle once in a newsreel about the army," Rebecca said. "I didn't know there would be one at camp." She slid from her bunk onto the bare wooden floor. "Morning, Tina," she said with a yawn. When there was no reply, Rebecca peeked into the bottom bed. It was empty, the covers pulled taut. Maybe Tina was changing in the outhouse again.

Ginny stepped into the tent. "Good morning, girls! Put on your bathing outfits and go have a wash in the pond. It's a cold dip, but it will wake you right up."

The girls dressed, grabbed soap, and straggled to the pond. Rebecca felt the chill air against her bare legs. She had never taken a bath like this before!

"Last one in is a skunk!" Cammie shouted, splashing into the water. The rest of the Beavers rushed in, yelping as the cold water hit them. They washed quickly, rinsed their hair with a fast dunk, and dashed back to the tent.

In dry clothes, the girls clamored for space in front of the cloudy piece of metal that served as a makeshift mirror. It was nailed to a tree above an outdoor washbasin. Rebecca tried to peer at herself as she combed her tangled hair.

"Braids would feel cooler," Ginny suggested. "If you girls team up, no one will need a mirror."

Rebecca braided Dottie's damp hair tightly, and Dottie returned the favor. The girls admired each other. As they hung their dripping suits on a rope strung between the trees, Ginny turned toward the dining hall. "Head for breakfast when you're done," she said. "I'll save a table."

As soon as Ginny was gone, Corky put her

hands on her hips and asked, "Where's Teeny?" The girls looked around, baffled. "Well, if the last one into the pond is a skunk, I guess we'll smell her before we see her," Corky said. She pinched her nose and added in a nasal voice, "And the smell won't be teeny at all!"

"What I smell is fried onions and potatoes," Josie said. "Let's eat!"

As the Beavers headed off in a ragtag group, they passed some younger girls scurrying toward the Crane tent with dripping watering cans.

"What on earth are you doing?" Bertie asked as the girls began pouring water on their tent stakes.

The Crane girls looked serious. "Why, the campers in Loon told us we have to keep the stakes wet or the tent will fall over," one explained. "Didn't you water yours?"

Rebecca was puzzled. "We'd better ask Ginny about that."

Josie nodded. "She's in the dining hall."

As soon as the Beavers left the watering can

brigade behind, Corky burst out laughing. "I can't believe they fell for that old trick."

"It's a trick?" Dottie asked. "But what if the stakes do dry out?"

Corky smirked. "It's a camp prank. They'll figure it out soon enough. My tent was fooled last year. We sure felt silly!"

In the meal line, Rebecca was amazed at the variety of food. There were heaping bowls of fried potatoes, scrambled eggs, bananas and oranges, breakfast rolls, pitchers of orange juice and milk, platters of pancakes—and sliced strawberries! She wondered if Tina had actually persuaded the cook to serve them. She spooned a pile onto her plate and then hesitated at a tray of curly strips of meat. "What's this?" she asked Corky.

"Ain't you ever eaten bacon?" Corky responded.

Ginny corrected Corky's grammar. "*Haven't* you ever eaten bacon," she repeated.

"Sure an' I've eaten it," Corky said, not real-izing her mistake. Ginny let it go.

Now that Rebecca knew what the meat was, she moved on. Although her family was willing to overlook the fact that food at camp didn't follow the Jewish *kosher* food laws, there was no reason for her to eat pork. It was strictly forbidden, and there were so many other dishes, she wouldn't go hungry.

Corky nudged Rebecca's arm. "Go ahead and try it, Beckie. It's delicious."

"My family doesn't eat that," Rebecca explained.

"Well, here's your chance," Corky said. "They'll never know." She dropped a few strips onto Rebecca's plate.

"No thanks," Rebecca said. She slid the bacon onto Corky's plate. Ginny shepherded the Beaver girls to a table. Tina was already seated, dressed in her long jumper, with a full plate of food in front of her.

Corky picked up a piece of bacon with her fingers and took a crunchy bite. "I can't believe Beckie passed up the best food of all."

"Different families have different ways of

doing things," Ginny said. "Why, Corky, I'll bet you wouldn't be eating that bacon if today were Friday, would you?"

"Of course not," Corky answered. "You can't eat meat on Fridays, now, can you?"

"That's the custom in Catholic families," Ginny explained, "but not everyone has the same religion." She smiled. "Now you and Rebecca have both learned something new."

"I think *she* should learn to eat what's put in front of her," Corky mumbled with her mouth full. Then she turned her attention to Tina. "And where were *you* this morning? You missed your bath." Rebecca was startled by Corky's bluntness, but she was curious about Tina, too.

"I...I'm...the bugler," Tina said, clearly flustered.

"So you're the culprit who blasted us awake," Sunny teased.

Josie was a bit grumpier. "I thought I was in the army!"

"Now, now, there's no need for teasing," Ginny interrupted. "Let's treat one another the same way we'd like to be treated."

Rebecca patted her bunk mate on the back. "Sounding the bugle is a hard job! Who else would get up that early?" Tina smiled gratefully.

The girls looked up as Roger sauntered in, his hair neatly slicked back. The hot food was already gone, but Roger walked right into the kitchen and came out in a few minutes with a full plate of bacon, eggs, and potatoes.

"Will ya look at that?" Cammie marveled. "I thought Miss Pepper was tough, but she must have a soft spot for Roger." Ginny looked up and her gaze lingered on Roger for a long moment.

"Looks like Miss Pepper's not the only one," Corky teased. Her eyes sparkled as she looked from Roger to Ginny.

Ginny ignored the remark and quickly took a list from her pocket. "All right, Beavers, here are your assignments this morning." She started reading. "Corky, please draw a bucket of fresh water and leave it at the washstand. Josie, please sweep out the tent. There's a broom standing in the corner. Tina, you'll collect napkins from the tables." She read off the chores until she got to the end. "Beckie, Miss Pepper needs a stack of kindling for the stove." The girls started removing their plates. "Be quick, now. Flag-raising begins in twenty minutes."

The campers scattered to complete their chores. Rebecca hurried into the kitchen and asked Miss Pepper where she might find the woodpile.

The cook barely glanced at her. "Just fill the bucket from the pile out back," she said impatiently as she strode into the dining hall.

Rebecca looked around the kitchen but didn't see a wood bucket. She noticed a closed door and wondered if the bucket might be behind it. The door opened to a dim pantry filled with sacks of flour and sugar, containers of oats, jars of pickles, and crates of bananas. A three-legged stool stood in a corner, and propped against the wall behind it was a pair of wooden crutches. Suddenly, a sharp voice startled her.

"Skedaddle!" Miss Pepper scolded. The

cook had returned to the kitchen lugging a pan of dirty dishes. Rebecca couldn't believe how quickly she put the dishpan down and slammed the pantry door shut. "What do you think you're doing poking around in there?"

"I'm just looking for the wood b—" Rebecca began, but Miss Pepper cut her off.

"Skedaddle!" she snapped again. She shooed at Rebecca with flapping hands as if Rebecca were a bothersome cat.

Rebecca returned to the dining hall, wondering how she would finish her chore. Tina had just collected an armful of napkins. "Miss Pepper kicked me out of the kitchen," Rebecca told her. "I couldn't find the wood bucket. Now I'll never be done in time."

"Check behind the stove," Tina suggested.

Rebecca cautiously opened the kitchen door and stepped in. Sure enough, the bucket was right where Tina had thought it might be. She grabbed it and hurried outside, filling it from a neat pile of kindling. She replaced the full bucket in its spot. Miss Pepper was at the sink, up to her elbows in soapy water. She ignored Rebecca completely.

Rebecca hurried to join Tina at the flagpole. "You were right about the bucket!" Rebecca told her. "How'd you know where it was?"

Tina whispered, "Just a lucky guess." The girls placed their hands over their hearts.

"The cook is a real grouch," Rebecca whispered back. "I wonder if Pepper is her real name, or if she earned it by being so crabby." She chuckled at her own joke, but Tina was already reciting the Pledge of Allegiance. Then they sang "America the Beautiful."

Rebecca found herself humming the tune as she went about her morning activities. At Crafts, she sat beside Tina at a large table. Babs passed out squares of felt to make name signs for their cubbies. "I'm going to write 'Beckie' with a sun instead of a dot over the *i*," Rebecca decided. "What about you?"

Corky leaned over and said, in a voice just low enough that Babs wouldn't hear, "She's going to write her name, 'Teeny.'"

Tina turned her back on Corky and said to Rebecca, "I think I'll put a moon over the i in my name. Let's get cubbies next to each other, and we'll be the sun and the moon."

"Oh, that's a great idea," Rebecca agreed.

Babs held up a brown sack. "Miss Pepper has given us some empty burlap bags," she said, "and you're going to make them into beautiful Indian dresses for the Hiawatha performance." The girls' eyes widened. "You can decorate your dresses with paint or embroidered designs. When you finish, I'll teach you to bead leather headbands. You're all going to be lovely maidens!"

Following Babs's directions, each girl cut holes in her sack for her head and arms, and then pulled away some of the loose threads at the bottom to make a fringe. Rebecca decided to embroider her dress with a design of waves and a beaming sun. Maybe that would bring good luck in learning to swim and paddle a canoe.

The girls chatted and stitched. "I'd love to be the narrator for our performance," Rebecca confided to Tina.

Corky butted in. "Last year I was the narrator for our performance, so I expect I'll do it again. After all, it's the most important role, and I have the most experience."

Rebecca was surprised. Wouldn't Ginny hold an audition to see who was the best narrator? *And if she does,* Rebecca mused, *don't I have as good a chance as anyone to win the role?*

4
MAKING A SPLASH

Rebecca folded her burlap dress, put it into her cubby, and skipped along the path toward the Beaver tent. A darting movement on the ground caught her attention. A small brown creature with white and black stripes down its back scampered across the trail, holding a berry in its mouth.

"A chipmunk!" Rebecca exclaimed. She had seen a drawing of one in a library book but had never seen a real one before. The chipmunk dashed under the porch on the main building, its tail held aloft like a flag. Rebecca squatted down, trying to spot it. As she peered under the porch, she heard Mr. Dee's high-pitched voice. "Do be more cautious, Hildegarde. What if the health committee shows up to inspect the camp?

If she's here eating a snack, they're bound to ask questions."

"Oh, don't make a big kerfuffle about it!" came Miss Pepper's voice. "I'll be sure no one sees. She needs to build up her strength."

The cook's name is Hildegarde? Rebecca marveled. She stifled a giggle.

"It's too risky," Mr. Dee argued. "And get rid of those crutches, too."

Whatever are they talking about? Rebecca wondered. She stood to go and nearly bumped into Tina, who had just stepped off the open porch.

"Oh!" Tina exclaimed. "What are you doing down there?"

"I was watching the cutest little chipmunk," Rebecca said, "but it's gone now. What are *you* doing here?"

Tina shrugged. "Just looking for something to do," she said.

"I just overheard the funniest thing," said Rebecca, breaking into a grin. "Mr. Dee called Miss Pepper *Hildegarde*—and she's trying to keep something a secret! Let's snoop around and find out what she's hiding."

Tina looked anxious. "We'd better not. I know—let's see if we can borrow the Hiawatha book. We can look through it to find a passage for our performance. That's going to be the best fun!"

"Good idea," Rebecca agreed. "It would give me a chance to practice a little, too. I know Corky thinks she's going to be the narrator, but I want to try out for that role, too. Just because Corky did it last year doesn't mean she has to do it again this year, does it?"

With the book in hand, the girls sat together on Tina's bunk in the deserted tent. "Gosh," Rebecca said, pushing back farther, "it's swell under here, Tina. It feels like a little hideaway."

"I do like it here," Tina said. "And Beckie? Thanks for not calling me Teeny like some of the other girls. I can't help it if I'm small."

"I'd never tease you like that," Rebecca said. "Come on, let's find a good passage to act out."

After lunch, Ginny called a tent meeting. "The performance night will be here before you know it," she told the girls, "so we need to choose a passage and choose roles."

Rebecca waved her hand in the air. "Tina and I looked through the book, and we think the very beginning would be the best part to act out. It starts with Nokomis and Hiawatha, and there are lots of forest animals and a hunting adventure."

"Nifty," Josie said. "That way our tent will get to perform first!" The other girls nodded enthusiastically.

"It seems we're all in agreement," Ginny said. "Let's take turns reading the passage aloud and decide on a narrator. Then we'll choose the other roles." She turned to Rebecca. "Since it was your suggestion, Beckie, why don't you start?"

Rebecca drew on all she had learned about acting. She spoke in a dramatic voice and paused in just the right places as she read:

By the shores of Gitchee Gumee,
By the shining Big-Sea-Water,
Stood the wigwam of Nokomis,
Daughter of the moon, Nokomis.
Dark behind her rose the forest,
Rose the black and gloomy pine trees,
Rose the firs with cones upon them;
Bright before it beat the water,
Beat the clear and sunny water,
Beat the shining Big-Sea-Water.

While she read the lines, Rebecca pictured the dark and mysterious pine forest and the pond glistening in the sunlight.

"Gee, Beckie, that was tip-top!" Bertie exclaimed.

"You should be our narrator," Tina said, her eyes shining. "Who could possibly read it better?"

Rebecca flushed with pride and excitement. Would she be chosen?

"That was a lovely reading," Ginny said. "Who else wants to give it a try?"

Corky reached for the book. "Last year when I was the narrator, everyone thought I did a swell job." She began reading. Her tone was flat, and she stumbled over the Indian names. "At the door on summer evenings, Sat the little Ha... Hawa... Oh, it's Hiawatha!" When she reached the end of the page, she handed Ginny the book.

Corky couldn't have been a narrator last year, Rebecca thought. *She doesn't even recognize Hiawatha's name!*

"Would anyone else like to read?" Ginny asked.

"I'd never want to read aloud," Dottie said. "I'd rather be a rabbit." The other girls murmured their agreement.

Rebecca crossed her fingers. *I read with more expression,* she couldn't help thinking. *I didn't miss a single word—not even Gitchee Gumee.*

Ginny was quiet for a moment, looking thoughtful. "It's difficult for me to choose between you," she said at last. She turned to Corky. "Since you were a narrator last year, let's give Beckie a turn."

The girls applauded. "Beckie! Beckie!" they cheered. Rebecca's heart leaped. She was going to be the narrator!

Corky's face turned as red as her flaming hair. "What am I going to play, then?" she sputtered.

"I think you'd be wonderful as Nokomis," Ginny said, "but you can decide. There are still many roles to fill, so think about which one you'd like."

Corky narrowed her eyes and glowered at Rebecca. The anger in her expression made Rebecca squirm.

That afternoon, the girls got ready for their first swimming lesson. Tina emerged from the outhouse in a bathing dress that was far too large. Instead of having bare legs like the rest of the girls, she wore droopy wool stockings. Poor Tina—Rebecca wondered why the City Children's Society hadn't given her proper-sized clothes. But Tina didn't seem bothered. She linked her arm through Rebecca's, and the two girls ambled down to the pond. Tina walked slowly, and Rebecca noticed she was limping. "Did you hurt your leg?" Rebecca asked.

Tina shrugged. "It happened a while ago."

"My cousin hurt his leg on the boat to America," Rebecca told her. "He fell and cut himself so badly that the doctors on Ellis Island almost sent him back to Russia! They thought a lame person wouldn't be able to take care of himself."

Tina's face clouded. "That's not right," she said quietly.

"My feelings exactly," Rebecca agreed. "Luckily, my cousin was able to stay, but it took a long time before his leg was completely healed."

Corky stepped up behind them. "So, it's the Eager Beavers," she taunted. "I suppose you two cooked up a plan to make Beckie the narrator, didn't you."

"May I have your full attention, girls," Roger called before Rebecca could reply. "You'll all learn to swim by the end of the session as long as you follow my instructions." He stood in the water, facing them, and began tossing out terms that Rebecca had never heard before. "You'll start with the dead man's float," he said, checking off each skill on his fingers, "and of course, treading water. You'll learn the dog paddle, and finally the crawl." Then Roger said the magic words Rebecca was waiting to hear. "Once you pass a test of basic water skills, we'll take a canoe trip." Rebecca eyed the sleek boats bobbing on the water's edge and imagined gliding across the pond.

"Before you step into the water," said Roger sternly, "there are some rules about water safety. First, no one goes into the pond without my permission. Second, always—"

A sharp elbow jabbed into Rebecca's back. She flailed her arms, trying to regain her balance, but found herself tumbling off the dock into the water. Rebecca gasped as the cold water hit her full force. Roger held her arm as she struggled to stand. Her feet sank into the squishy mud, and she wiped away the water streaming down her face. The girls on the dock roared with laughter.

Corky grinned. "Roger sure can dodge like a champion. I guess he's Roger Dodger!"

Roger was not laughing, and neither was Rebecca. He checked to be certain she was unhurt and then frowned. "I meant it when I said no one is ever to enter the water without my signal." He pointed to shore. "Young lady, out of the water. There will be no swimming for you today."

"Somebody pushed me," Rebecca protested. Corky looked at Rebecca and shook her head in sympathy, but Rebecca saw the hint of a smile. She felt certain Corky had shoved her, perhaps because she was angry that Rebecca had been chosen as narrator. *But I earned the role, fair and square!* thought Rebecca.

Roger scanned the faces of the Beaver girls lined up on the dock. "Who's responsible?" he asked, studying each of the girls in turn. He paused momentarily when he looked at Tina, and Rebecca thought she saw Tina give a slight nod in Corky's direction, but she wasn't sure.

"Corky," Roger said, "come forward, please." Corky smirked as she stepped to the edge of the dock. "I believe you have an apology to make to Rebecca for that little prank, and to everyone else for disrupting the lesson."

"Me?" Corky said innocently. "But—"

Roger held up his hand. "No excuses, and no horseplay. Waterfront rules are too important to be broken. Both of you, out!" Rebecca waded ashore dripping wet. Corky pouted and stalked off the dock. They each slumped down on the beach facing opposite directions.

"If I miss my lesson, how will I pass the swim test?" Rebecca snapped at Corky's back. "There aren't many days to learn all the strokes."

"You'll manage, I'm sure," Corky muttered. "Don't you always get what you want?"

Rebecca was too upset to argue anymore. Her face burned with embarrassment at being scolded in front of the others. Glumly, she watched the lesson. Tina was swimming the length of the dock with strong, smooth strokes, her head bobbing in and out of the water as she took regular breaths of air.

When the lesson was over, Corky left in a huff. Rebecca walked back to the tent with Tina. "You sure are a good swimmer," Rebecca remarked. "Did you have lessons before?" She added, "I'll never catch up."

Tina took her hand. "It's easy," she said, "and Roger's a good teacher. Tomorrow I'll show you what you missed."

Rebecca felt better knowing she could count on Tina. That's what friends were for.

That night the campers gathered in the clearing at sundown. The water reflected an orange glow from the setting sun. Slowly, the sky darkened, turning the treetops to a black silhouette. Sparks of dancing light appeared in the air.

"Look!" Rebecca said, pointing into the dusk. "They're like tiny stars all around us."

"Fireflies," Tina murmured. "I love them. My

mother says they're sparkles of love in the night."

Rebecca was charmed by Tina's description. "Why, I've never seen anything like this!"

"Me, neither," Josie said. "There aren't any fireflies in the Lower East Side! Where did you see them before, Tina? In Central Park?" Before Tina could answer, Roger lit the campfire.

"Tell us another scary story," begged one of the campers from the Deer tent.

"A *windigo* story," piped up another girl. "Please?"

Roger walked slowly around the fire circle. "Not so long ago," he began, "a windigo stalked the forests around us, looking for humans to satisfy its hunger. The Indians traveled in bands so they wouldn't be caught alone. They kept their children close to the wigwams. But sometimes, even children had to go into the forest to gather wood for the cooking fires."

He paused and looked out at the pitch-black forest. "One bright day, two sisters set off to collect kindling. Suddenly, the sky grew as dark as night, and the wind began to howl." Roger made a howling sound as he said the word. He dropped his voice dramatically. "The girls felt a chill creeping into their bones. With their arms loaded with sticks, they hurried home."

Rebecca shivered. She snuggled close to Sunny and Tina as Roger continued. "Just as the girls came to the end of the path, a heap of boulders blocked the trail. As they skirted the rocks, they heard a frightful *hiss, hiss, hiss!*" Roger leaned close to groups of girls, hissing. "Suddenly, a low rumble made the earth tremble, and a skeleton-like monster rose up from the boulders. Its eyes were sunk deep in its skull, and sharp fangs protruded from its lipless mouth." Firelight shadowed the campers' faces, their eyes wide.

"The sisters ran toward their wigwam," Roger said, "throwing their sticks into the monster's path. It slipped and slid, tumbling to earth with a terrifying *thump!*" Roger banged his fist against a bench, startling them all. "Into the wigwam they ran, pulling the bark covering closed. They crouched behind the fire as a long, bony arm reached in through the flaps and grabbed one sister's shoulder!" As Roger uttered these words, he reached over and clutched Ginny's shoulder. She jumped and let out a squeal. The girls gasped in surprise.

"Then what happened?" they asked.

Roger went on. "That clever maiden lifted a hot coal from the fire with a forked stick and tossed it right into the windigo's gaping mouth. It let out a shriek—much louder than Ginny's—and vanished in a cloud of mist. The sisters heard its piercing moan echo through the forest." Roger dropped his voice to a raspy whisper, as if confiding a secret. "Folks around here say that very windigo still lives among the rocks, and sometimes, on a still night, they hear its chilling cry." Roger looked from face to face around the circle. "So, late at night, if you hear a howl in the woods—*beware!*"

Rebecca's mouth went dry. She hugged Sunny and turned to pull Tina closer, but her place was empty. Rebecca scanned the circle of campers. Tina was gone.

5
THE TRUNK

"Where's Tina?" Rebecca asked Sunny.

"I don't know. I never saw her leave." Sunny turned to Cammie. "Have you seen Tina?"

"No, but I'd be afraid to go anywhere alone after that story," Cammie admitted.

Corky leaned in toward the others. "Maybe the windigo grabbed her!"

"Don't be silly," said Rebecca, trying to sound unconcerned. But why would Tina leave the circle?

The campers joined hands and swayed as they sang "Taps." Then they filed to their tents by the light of the oil lanterns. When Rebecca entered the Beaver tent, there was Tina, nestled under her blanket.

"Oh, you're here!" she exclaimed. "Why

didn't you tell us you were leaving? We were
worried about you."

"I—I was tired," she said.

"Weren't you nervous walking back by
yourself—in the dark?" asked Cammie, but
Tina just shrugged.

"Gosh, Ginny, you sure jumped a mile when
Roger grabbed you," Josie teased.

Ginny blushed. "He startled me all right.
That Roger sure can spin a tale."

"*Hissssss...*" Josie breathed, imitating Roger
and reaching out to grab the other girls. They
shrank away from her, laughing and pushing
against the tent walls.

"That's enough," Ginny laughed, "before you
pull the whole tent down!" She settled on the
camp stool. "I can see that Roger's got you all
riled up." She thumbed through the Hiawatha
book. "Let me find a passage to get you all to
sleep. Ah, here's a nice one."

Ginny read in a soothing voice, and again
Rebecca could picture the scene in her mind.
The passage ended with the lines,

Wah-wah-taysee, little firefly,
Little, flitting, white-fire insect,
Little, dancing, white-fire creature,
Light me with your little candle,
Ere upon my bed I lay me,
Ere in sleep I close my eyelids.

Rebecca pictured real fireflies blinking like stars that had drifted to earth. That was a much more comforting image to end the day with than Roger's windigo rising from a heap of boulders. She hugged her pillow. The other campers whispered together in their bunks amid muffled giggles. Rebecca suddenly missed Rose. "Tell me about the things you like to do, and where you live," she whispered down to Tina.

"I'm probably not much different from you, except I don't have any brothers or sisters," Tina whispered back. "It must be nifty to have a big family."

Rebecca told Tina about her twin sisters, Sadie and Sophie, and confessed how she envied all the privileges they had now that they were sixteen. She chattered about her bossy older brother, Victor, and her little brother, Benny, who was seven. "He's pretty cute," she said, "but he can be a real pest." Then Rebecca told Tina about her cousin Max and his wife, Lily, who were real movie actors in California. "Now it's your turn. Tell me about your family," she said, but Tina didn't say a word. Rebecca leaned over the edge of her bunk and peered down. Tina's eyes were closed and she was breathing deeply. Rebecca sighed. She had talked too long—her bunk mate was fast asleep.

A creaking sound nearby awakened Rebecca as daylight began to chase the darkness from the tent. She blinked her eyes in the dusky light and raised her head. The other girls were still sleeping, but Tina knelt beside her open trunk, dressed in the jumper she wore each morning. She lifted a bulky canvas bag out of the trunk.

What on earth was it? Rebecca hoped to see Tina open the bag, but instead she carried it to her bunk, disappearing from view. Rebecca heard a muffled *clink*, and then again, *clink*.

Tina leaned over the trunk and dropped an empty canvas bag inside, and then she pulled out the bugle and set it carefully on the floor. Silently she closed the lid of the trunk and looped the twine through the latch, tying it tightly. Whatever had been inside the mysterious bag must have been left on her bed, out of sight. Rebecca barely heard Tina leave the tent, as silent as the sunrise.

Rebecca slipped from her bunk and saw that Tina's bedding was pulled tight. There wasn't a hint of anything left behind. Rebecca turned to the trunk, curious. The knotted twine looked forbidding, but perhaps she could untie it and peek inside. Tina was gone, so she'd never know. What would be the harm in just looking?

Treat one another as you would wish to be treated, Ginny had advised them. Rebecca hesitated. She knew that she would be upset if someone snooped into her carpetbag. Rebecca stared at the trunk as if trying to see through the top.

I could just lift the lid a smidgen, she thought. *I wouldn't touch anything.* In spite of her misgivings, she reached for the knotted twine. Just as her fingers closed over it, the bugle call blasted through the air. Rebecca jumped back, as if she had been caught snooping. She scrambled back into bed as her tent mates stretched awake.

6
HUNTING FOR CHOKES

At breakfast, Tina was already at the table waiting to eat. Neither the mysterious contents of the bag nor the bugle were anywhere in sight. Although Tina couldn't possibly know what she had almost done, Rebecca avoided Tina's eyes. She was relieved when Josie suggested that they take a hike along some new trails.

"We could climb up the hill past the main lodge," Corky said. "There's a pretty view of the pond from the top."

Ginny looked hesitant. "I offered to help Babs with some props for the show," she said. "I expected you'd all be at the Crafts tent with me."

"We'll be fine on our own," Corky said confidently. "I know the way from last year."

"Oh, please let us go," begged Josie, her

hands folded as if in prayer.

"If I let you hike on your own, you must promise to stick together and stay on the trail," Ginny warned them. "I don't want you lost in the woods!"

"Or captured by a windigo," Dottie said with a forced laugh as the girls scattered to complete their chores.

As Rebecca carried serving dishes from the table into the kitchen, she noticed an empty oatmeal carton lying on the wooden counter. The round container gave her an idea. She cautiously approached Miss Pepper. "Um . . . I was just wondering," Rebecca stammered, "can I—I mean, *may* I—have this for our performance? It would make a nifty drum."

"It's always good to use something twice," Miss Pepper said. She wiped out the container with a damp cloth and handed it to Rebecca. "It's all yours," she said.

Maybe Miss Pepper isn't so grumpy after all, Rebecca thought happily as she raced to the Crafts tent and stuffed the container into her cubby. Then she hurried to flag-raising.

Two campers from Loon sauntered over as the Beavers gathered for their hike. "We heard you were taking a tramp," one of them said, "and we're all dreaming of chokeberries. If you pick some, we can share them at lunch." They held out two straw baskets.

"I've heard of choke*cherries*," said Cammie. "Are these the same thing?"

"Not really," said the other Loon girl.

"How can we find something we've never seen?" Josie asked.

"Don't worry," a Loon girl reassured her. "Chokes are pretty easy to spot."

Cammie and Dottie each took a basket, and the girls headed off on the trail, walking in pairs behind Corky. At first, Tina hung back. "Aren't you coming?" Rebecca asked. "Come on, you're my partner." Tina hesitated a moment, then took Rebecca's hand and stepped onto the path.

"This will be an adventure!" Rebecca said. She made up a silly chant. "We're off for chokes, we're off for chokes, 'cause Beavers are the

smartest folks!" The other girls chimed in.
Along the way, they stopped to check small
bushes and wild vines but found no berries.

The path led them alongside a tranquil
stream. Josie bent down and scooped something
up. "I think I found a salamander!" she called.
The others crowded around. Josie opened her
hands to reveal a shiny orange creature squirm-
ing in her hands.

"Ooh, put it down," Dottie cried. "What if
it bites?" Josie studied the creature thoroughly
before setting it back on the ground. She watched
until it disappeared under the wet leaves.

As the girls climbed higher up the hill,
Rebecca noticed that Tina was limping. "Is your
leg hurting?" she asked quietly, slowing to keep
pace with her bunk mate.

Just then, Corky gave a shout. "Look at this!"
She pointed to a vine snaking up a tree trunk.

"Is that a chokeberry vine?" Rebecca asked.

"It might be," Corky said. "Why don't you
pick a few leaves, and we'll show them to the
Loonies. They'll know if it's the right plant."

"I don't see any berries," remarked Rebecca, reaching to check underneath the leaves.

"Don't touch it, Beckie!" Tina yelled. "That's poison ivy. Touch it and you'll get a rash that'll make you itch like the devil!" She glared at Corky. "You knew that from *last year,* didn't you?" The girls backed away from the vine.

"Just teasing," Corky said with a forced smile. "I wouldn't have really let anyone touch it."

Rebecca glared at Corky. Then she turned to Tina and said, "Thanks for saving me. How did you know that was poison ivy?"

Tina shrugged. "I don't know. I think I saw it in a book somewhere."

"That's how I knew about salamanders," Josie said. "But I never thought I'd be lucky enough to find a real one!"

"Come on," Bertie said. "Let's keep searching."

"Right," Corky agreed. "If we split up, we'll find the berries twice as fast."

"But we promised Ginny we'd stay together," Bertie argued.

HUNTING FOR CHOKES

Corky ignored the reminder. She pointed to a trail leading toward a sun-splashed meadow where the wind rippled the tall grass. "Josie, Cammie, Sunny, and I will go that way. The rest of you stay on this trail. If we find the berries, I'll give a whistle." Corky stuck two fingers in her mouth and gave a piercing whistle to demonstrate. She turned to the girls she had chosen. "Stick with me, lassies," she said and marched off with the three campers following dutifully behind.

Bertie, Dottie, Tina, and Rebecca tried to follow the path as it wound deeper into the forest. Suddenly, two narrow trails branched off in different directions. "Which way?" Bertie asked.

Trees blocked the sunlight, casting gloomy shadows. "This is the forest primeval," Rebecca intoned, quoting Longfellow.

Dottie shivered. "Cut it out, Beckie."

Tina slumped down on a fallen log. "I've had enough of this. I've never even heard of chokeberries."

"None of us have," Bertie said, swinging the empty basket. "That's why they're hard to find."

"Come on, Tina," Rebecca coaxed, "let's find them before Corky's team does!"

Tina shook her head. "You go ahead. I'll wait here for you."

Rebecca suspected that Tina's leg was hurting and she didn't want to admit it. "All right, you stay here and we'll just search a little farther up the path," she said.

A cool breeze pushed them along as the path twisted and turned. The three girls tramped left and right, trying to stay on the trail, but it soon faded into the leaf litter and disappeared. At the top of a slope, they stopped to get their bearings. Before them, a mound of rocks blocked the way.

Dottie pointed to a shadowy opening under a large boulder. "Look—it's just like the rocks in Roger's story," she breathed.

"That's just made-up," Rebecca said, "but this looks like a real cave! Come on, let's explore it. Corky and her gang will be so jealous when they hear about it." She clambered down the rocks closer to the entrance. Bertie followed behind, while Dottie hung back. Rebecca stepped inside. "The rocks on the wall glitter," she reported. "It's amazing!"

Bertie lingered at the opening and Dottie looked frightened. "Let's go back, Beckie," she pleaded. "I'm scared."

Just as Rebecca was about to reassure Dottie, a low sound echoed from deep inside— whoooshh! It wafted toward them on the shifting breeze.

Bertie's face paled. "It's the windigo cave!" she squealed. She grabbed Rebecca's hand, and the trio dashed back in the direction they had come. Blindly, they ran through the underbrush until they were panting and breathless. At last, they burst out of the woods into a welcome patch of sunlight. They blinked into the sudden brightness and looked around. There was no sign of the trail.

"We're lost!" Dottie groaned. "And what about Tina?"

"Maybe we can find the others," Rebecca said, trying to sound hopeful. She cupped her hands to her mouth and called, "*Co-o-or–ky! Ti-i-i–na!*" She listened for an answering shout, or Corky's whistle, but the only sound was a raucous blue jay screeching overhead.

The girls walked in circles, searching for the trail without success. Rebecca's mouth felt dry, and she began to worry. They shouldn't have left Tina alone.

Dottie's voice quivered. "We'll never find them. We don't even know where we are."

The gurgle of water tumbling over stones caught Rebecca's ear. She pushed through a cluster of bushes until she saw the stream they had followed on the tramp into the woods. "I think if we follow along the bank, the stream will lead us back to camp," Rebecca said.

"Let's try it," Bertie agreed.

The girls trudged along, worrying about Tina, Corky, and the others who were still somewhere back in the woods. After a long tramp, the girls straggled into camp, hot and tired.

"Let's find Ginny," Rebecca said.

The girls went directly to the Crafts tent. As they stepped inside, they were startled to see Corky and the rest of the Beavers making small bark canoes. Tina sat on a stool, neatly stitching the edges of the white bark.

"Saints preserve us!" Corky exclaimed. "What took you so long?"

Ginny looked worried and cross. "I warned you all to stay together. Corky told me that you insisted on going off on your own."

Bertie pointed to Corky and her group. "They're the ones who left us!"

Rebecca looked toward Tina, hoping her bunk mate would vouch for their story, but Tina just bent her head over her stitching.

Dottie added, "We got lost—and then we heard the windigo hissing in a cave. We were so scared, we ran into the woods and thought we'd never get back!"

Ginny's eyebrows lifted. "Now, girls," she chided them, "you're making up tales."

"Oh, no," Rebecca said earnestly. "We heard

it. There was a real cave, and a creepy sound coming out of it."

Ginny's annoyance seemed to disappear. "I've heard there's a cave around here. I'll bet that's what you found. We should tramp out there for a little exploration. Caves are interesting places."

"I'm never going anywhere near there again!" Dottie declared.

"Me neither," agreed Rebecca. "Besides, we don't even know where it was, we were so lost."

The tent flap opened, and one of the Loons poked her head in. "Who got the chokes?"

Dottie handed over the empty basket. Her face was flushed with the heat. "We couldn't find a single chokeberry."

"Wait a minute!" the older girl exclaimed. "Did you say *choke*berries?" She pressed her hand to her throat and gasped as if she were choking. Then she grinned. "We said *joke*berries! And the joke's on you!"

Behind her, several Loons doubled over in laughter. Ginny shook her head and rolled her eyes. Corky and the girls she had taken with her snickered.

Rebecca felt her suspicion growing. She confronted Corky. "You knew it was a prank all along, didn't you? And instead of telling us, you left us out in the woods!"

"I've been here before, remember?" Corky boasted. "I think my friends appreciated the voice of experience."

Waves of hot anger washed over Rebecca. She had wasted the entire morning tramping through the woods because of a silly prank, and had been scared half to death to boot.

"I never should have let you girls hike on your own," Ginny said. She ushered Rebecca, Bertie, and Dottie outside. "You get a good drink of water and then hurry back. I'll show you how to make the canoes."

Fuming, Rebecca splashed water on her face and gulped a few handfuls before heading back to Crafts. Cutting a traced shape of a canoe from a folded strip of bark, she glanced at Tina. "I suppose you knew this was just a prank, too?"

"Honestly, I didn't," Tina murmured.

Rebecca started stitching the thick bark and pricked her finger. "Phooey!" she exclaimed. She was too upset to sew.

She dropped the unfinished canoe in her cubby and retrieved the oatmeal container. Sitting by herself, she glued a thin strip of birch bark around the outside and stretched a scrap of leather over the open end. She tied it tightly with heavy brown twine.

Tina stepped to her side. "Can I see what you're making?" she asked cautiously.

Rebecca tapped the drumhead and recited the opening lines in rhythm with the beats: "'By the shores of Gitchee-Gumee, By the shining Big-Sea-Water.'"

Tina smiled shyly. "A drum! It's wonderful. You're going to be the best narrator in the whole camp."

Rebecca couldn't help smiling as her sore feelings about the hike were replaced with excitement about the show. She glanced at the others to see if they liked the drum idea, too, but Corky and the girls beside her—Cammie, Josie, and Sunny—exchanged furtive glances and didn't utter a word.

7
MESSAGE FROM HOME

"Mail call!" Mr. Dee announced after lunch. Rebecca was delighted when she heard her name called. She pocketed a white envelope with Mama's neat handwriting and hurried to the tent.

"Any mail from home, Tina?" Rebecca asked as she climbed up to her bunk.

"I don't need a letter," Tina said. "I mean, I'll be home soon."

"I suppose so," Rebecca agreed, but she was delighted. This was the first letter she had ever received. She ran her finger over the stamp. Mama had spent two whole pennies to send it.

"So, it's mail we're getting," Corky said. "Aren't we important." Rebecca couldn't miss the jealousy in Corky's voice.

"You'll probably get mail tomorrow," Rebecca said kindly, determined to forgive what had happened on the hike that morning.

"Maybe—if my ma learns to read and write overnight," Corky retorted.

"Say, can I have the stamp?" Cammie asked, looking over Rebecca's shoulder at the envelope. "I'm starting a collection."

Rebecca hesitated. This was her very first letter—even the envelope seemed precious. "I'm sorry," she said, "but I'm saving it."

"You can have mine, Cammie," offered Sunny.

"Enough about mail," said Corky. She pulled out the stool Ginny used for evening reading and clapped her hands together. "It's meeting time!"

The other girls dropped what they were doing and gathered around, but Rebecca wanted to read her letter first. She slid her finger under the envelope flap and carefully lifted the seal. She slipped out the letter and read.

My dear Beckie,

The house feels too quiet without you. The whole family sends their greetings and hopes you are having fun. Benny wants you to bring him a real, live frog. We all laughed at the idea of you packing a jumping frog into your carpetbag!

We are well, although the polio outbreak in the city has grown worse. I've been keeping Benny indoors to be sure he doesn't catch it, but that's made him restless and full of mischief! I am relieved that you are away from all this illness and safe at camp.

Still, do remember to be careful of germs. Wash your hands as often as you can! We trust that the epidemic will be over soon, and look forward to having you home again.

Your loving Mama

"Come on, Beckie, pay attention!" Corky called.

Trying to hide her annoyance, Rebecca folded the letter back into the envelope and tucked it under her pillow. She would read it again when she was alone. It sounded as if things were even worse in the city than when she had left. She hoped that Rose was all right.

Rebecca picked up her drum and sat on the floor with the others. "My brother wants me to bring him a frog!" she told the girls, who giggled.

"Pooh," Corky scoffed. "Right now we need to talk about our *Hiawatha* presentation."

"Just wait till you hear how it sounds with a drumbeat!" Tina said.

Rebecca tapped her drum. "I've already memorized the entire passage."

Corky ignored them both. "*Last year* when we planned our show, everyone had a vote."

"But we don't have anything to vote on," Bertie pointed out.

"Indeed we do!" Corky exclaimed. "We let *someone* become the narrator without any vote at all. I say we take one now." She tossed her head and narrowed her green eyes. "All those in favor of *me* being the narrator, raise your hands."

To Rebecca's shock, Josie, Cammie, and Sunny raised their hands immediately. Then Corky raised her own hand high in the air. "That's four votes," she said. "One more would be a majority." She stared pointedly at Dottie. "Maybe from somebody who doesn't want to do everyone else's chores," she said ominously.

Dottie seemed to shrink down. Her eyes darted to Rebecca and shifted quickly away. She half-raised her arm, bent at the elbow.

"I can barely see that vote," Corky barked. Dottie slowly raised her arm a bit higher. Corky gave a tight smile. "Five votes—a clear majority. That's the fair way to do things."

Rebecca was stunned. Had Corky secretly plotted this? She must have convinced the girls to side with her when they followed her back to camp on the hike. But what about Dottie? "There's nothing fair about it!" Rebecca cried. "You're turning everyone against me!"

Corky reached for the drum. "Nifty," she said.

"That's mine!" Rebecca exclaimed. "I made it—"

"—for the narrator," Corky reminded her. "And that's me."

A beam of sunlight fell across the floor as Ginny stepped into the tent. Her dimples showed as she smiled and held up the Longfellow book. "Shall we practice for our performance?" She handed the book to Rebecca, but Corky grabbed it.

"I'll take that," she said. "We've taken a democratic vote, and the girls want me to be narrator after all."

Ginny arched her eyebrows in surprise. "Is that so?" She looked at Rebecca questioningly. Rebecca opened her mouth and then clamped it shut. She longed to protest, to tell Ginny about Corky's trick, but she didn't know where to begin. Besides, what could Ginny do now that there had been a vote? Rebecca's shoulders slumped with defeat, and she stared down at her lap.

"Well, if that's what you've decided," Ginny said slowly, "we've got even more work ahead of us than I imagined. Beckie, I guess you'll act out the role of grandmother Nokomis, then."

Rebecca was speechless with anger. How could this be happening? She'd already memorized the passage, and she had made the drum to beat the rhythm of the words. But the worst part was the sneaky way that Corky had gotten some of the girls to vote against her. And not one Beaver had protested—not even Tina.

For the rest of the day, Rebecca felt as if she were isolated in a bubble. She couldn't face her tent mates, and she barely listened to Roger's campfire story until his deep voice grabbed her attention at the end:

"The windigo rose from the mist and enveloped its victim, sucking his breath. In place of the gentle soul who once lived peacefully among his people, the windigo took over the human's body until he became a windigo, too."

Rebecca felt a shiver race up her back, and also a pang of loneliness as she realized she had no friend to huddle with tonight.

After lights-out, Tina gently poked Rebecca from the lower bunk. "Beckie, I'm sorry about what happened today," she said softly.

Rebecca was silent for a long moment. Finally she muttered, "If a windigo crept into Corky's body, how would we know the difference? She's already acting like a monster."

Tina laughed quietly, but Rebecca wasn't cheered up at all. "Tina—" Rebecca began. She stopped, and then blurted out, "Did you think the vote was fair?"

"No, but I was afraid to say a word," Tina confessed. "Besides, it wouldn't have done any good."

Rebecca felt a sour taste in her mouth. How would Tina know that if she hadn't even tried? Rebecca realized that although she thought of Tina as her friend, she barely knew her. Rebecca had shared stories about her own family, but Tina hadn't said anything about hers.

Rebecca listened to the other campers chatting back and forth until they fell asleep. She had thought that all the Beavers would be her friends, but now Corky had split them apart. Even Tina had let her down. True, she hadn't voted for Corky to be narrator, but she hadn't spoken against it, either. Rebecca rolled over to face the wall, fighting back tears. You were supposed to be able to depend on a friend.

As tired as she was, Rebecca couldn't sleep. It was partly the heat and partly trying to figure out how things at camp had gone so wrong. She kicked off her blanket. *Maybe if I splash some water on my face, I'll feel better,* she thought.

She crept from the tent and walked toward the washbasin, picking her way carefully in the dark. A sudden movement caught her eye, and she turned her head just in time to see a flowing white shadow gliding along the path ahead. Rebecca's heart raced, but curiosity held her to the spot. She called softly, "Who's there?" The only answer was the sound of crickets chirping and the rustle of pine trees in the light breeze.

Ta-whoo! Ta-whoo! A hooting sound pierced the air, exactly like the call she had heard the other night. The hair on Rebecca's neck prickled in fear. The call sounded closer and felt much spookier now that she was out alone. Rebecca tried to guess how far she was from the tent. Going to the washstand had been a dangerous idea.

Suddenly, the ghostly figure stepped back onto the path and moved toward her. It was much closer now! How did it move so fast? Rebecca turned and dashed for the tent. She couldn't waste a second to look behind her. Just as she reached the tent, a hand reached out and grabbed her.

8
A Slimy Trick

Rebecca squealed. *"Shhh!"* came a whispered voice. She looked up and saw that Ginny had collared her. The counselor wore her night shift, a long, flowing white chemise.

"Oh, you frightened me so!" Rebecca whispered.

"I didn't mean to scare you, but I didn't want to wake the others by calling out loud," Ginny said softly. "I came to make one last check of the tent before I went to bed—and you are breaking the rules."

Rebecca flinched at the accusation. "I couldn't sleep, and I just wanted to wash my face . . . and then I thought I saw a ghost on the path and heard a really scary sound!"

"I'm the ghost, apparently," Ginny said, "and

the sound you heard was probably just an owl. You wouldn't have been frightened if you'd been in bed where you belong."

"I...I'm sorry," Rebecca said. "I won't leave the tent at night ever again."

Ginny released her grip on Rebecca's shoulder. "Get back inside then," she said, "and get some sleep." She watched until Rebecca dropped the tent flaps closed.

In bed, Rebecca tossed and turned. She tried to feel reassured by Ginny's explanation, but that eerie hooting—could it really be an owl? Or was it something else?

The next morning, Rebecca felt tired from her restless night. After breakfast, she swept the tent sluggishly and then walked to flag-raising. Corky rushed into the circle just as they finished the Pledge of Allegiance. It wasn't like her to be late. Rebecca wondered what she had been up to, but was simply too tired to think about it.

On the beach, Rebecca perked up her ears as Roger explained canoe strokes. "This is the proper grip," he said, holding up a polished wooden paddle. In spite of herself, Rebecca yawned. Tina nudged her arm and made a questioning face, as if to ask why she was tired.

When Roger turned away to demonstrate how the paddle stroke looked from the back, Rebecca leaned toward Tina and asked quietly, "Did you hear strange sounds last night?"

Tina shook her head, but Corky's face turned pale under her freckles. "I heard an eerie hooting," she said under her breath. "And it wasn't the first time."

"Pay attention, girls," Roger's voice interrupted. Rebecca sat up straight.

Corky fidgeted. "I'm sorry, Roger Dodger, but some of us heard the windigo hooting last night."

Roger shook his finger at them. "You're supposed to be sleeping at night, not worrying about sounds in the forest."

Rebecca held her breath. Roger hadn't said

that they were imagining things, or even that the spooky sound was just an owl. Rebecca and Corky exchanged a glance. It was almost as if they shared a secret understanding. But Rebecca reminded herself that she couldn't trust Corky—not for a minute.

That afternoon when the Beavers rehearsed their performance, Corky read the poem haltingly, tripping over the rhythm and stumbling over words. She tried to keep a steady drumbeat, but that only slowed down her reading.

Rebecca mimed the role of Nokomis sitting on the shore. She pretended to rock the baby Hiawatha and then put him down and pointed to a comet in the sky. Suddenly, Corky slapped the book closed. She cocked her head critically. "Don't wave your arms around, Beckie. You look ridiculous."

"I don't need any advice from you," Rebecca snapped. "I don't know how you performed last summer, but *this year* you can't even read your part!"

Corky's shoulders slumped. "Wh–what do

you know?" she stammered. "I was really good—everyone said so!"

Rebecca was furious. "You don't know anything about acting! I was in a moving picture once, and I know more about it than you'll ever know!"

Corky gave a tight smile. "Fancy that! We've a movie star in our tent—or a fibber!" There was a brief outburst of nervous laughter, and Rebecca was especially stung to see Tina join in.

"Goodness, Teeny, why do you change in the outhouse all the time?" Corky griped that night. "Why can't you stay in the tent with everyone else?"

Tina rolled over in her bunk and didn't answer.

Rebecca ignored them both and got into bed. As she slid under her blankets, she felt something slimy against her bare foot. The cold, clammy feeling moved up her leg. She yelped and jumped up. Standing on the bare floor, Rebecca threw back the covers. A large frog with bulging eyes screeched and hopped off the bed, landing with a heavy *thump* on Tina's trunk. Josie giggled nervously while the other girls squealed and hung back.

"Saints preserve us!" Corky cried.

Tina grabbed the fat green frog in one swift motion. "It's just a harmless bullfrog," she said. "Poor thing!"

Corky quickly recovered her composure. "Sure an' your brother would love it," she said dryly to Rebecca. "Shall we pack it in your carpetbag?"

"Did you put that frog in my bed?" Rebecca demanded.

"I wouldn't go near a slimy thing like that," Corky said.

Ginny had come into the tent during the commotion. "What am I going to do with you girls?" she sighed. "I don't want any more pranks. Who's behind this?" The girls looked around, but no one confessed. Tina gently carried the frog outside.

Rebecca glared at Corky, and then glanced at Tina. Her bunk mate had picked up the frog without hesitation. Still, she couldn't believe Tina would play such a nasty trick. Rebecca looked at the other campers. A faint smile played across Cammie's face. Had she planted the frog because Rebecca wouldn't give her the stamp?

Ginny opened the Hiawatha book. "All right, then, everyone settle down. The excitement is over." Still, some of the girls peeked under their blankets before getting back into bed.

Rebecca pulled her covers all the way back, searching for any more hidden surprises. For the first time, she was truly homesick. She even missed her sisters. If only Rose were there with her! In spite of the other campers around her, without a true friend, Rebecca felt alone.

After Ginny bade the girls good night, Rebecca reached under her pillow for her mother's letter. At least she could read about home, even if she couldn't be there. She groped under the pillow but felt only the taut sheet. Sitting up, she lifted the pillow. She was certain she had left the letter there; where could it be? Had the person who put the frog in her bed taken the *letter*, too? Or was the missing letter just another prank?

In the faint moonlight, Rebecca scoured the folds of the blanket and sheets. Maybe the letter had fallen. She ran her hand between the mattress and the bed frame. But the letter wasn't there.

Rebecca felt a knot in the pit of her stomach. She squeezed her eyes closed as silent tears rolled down her cheeks and onto her pillow.

9
A PRIVATE PICNIC

"You're late again," Ginny scolded Corky after flag-raising. "You were late yesterday, as well."

"My chore took longer than I expected," Corky protested. "I won't miss flag-raising again."

"See that you don't," Ginny cautioned. Rebecca knew she shouldn't gloat, but she couldn't help feeling a tinge of satisfaction.

"Attention, Beaver girls!" Roger called. "Head to the waterfront for your swimming test."

Rebecca was elated. At last she could take the swimming test and earn a chance to take out a canoe. Then she felt a moment of panic. Was she ready? Different swimming strokes scrolled through her mind like a silent movie. *Dead man's* *float—close your eyes, hold your breath, **relax**. Back float—spread your arms, eyes up, let the water hold you, **relax.*** Lining up on the dock with the other campers, Rebecca kept as far from Corky as possible. She didn't want to be sent out of the water today, of all days.

"I really want to pass so that I can canoe," Bertie said.

"Me too," Rebecca agreed. "I've even been practicing in the mornings when we bathe. And Tina's been giving me some extra help."

Bertie glanced down the line of Beavers. "Speaking of Tina, I wonder where she is."

Doesn't Tina want to take the test so she can canoe? Rebecca wondered. Surely she'd pass easily. Where was she?

Roger put the girls through their paces, two at a time. When it was her turn, Rebecca waded into the water. She hated the squishy feel of the muddy pond bottom but loved the cool water against her skin.

"Back float," Roger commanded. Rebecca and Bertie leaned back and let the water hold them. Bravely Rebecca opened her eyes and stared at the clouds while gentle waves lapped around her face. Next, she paddled into deeper water and pumped her legs furiously to tread water. Roger held a stopwatch and timed them for two full minutes.

"Dog paddle," Roger called, and Rebecca thought that was almost too easy. Finally, the girls did a basic crawl from one end of the dock to the other. Rebecca was breathless, but she had made it!

"Two more Beaver paddlers," Roger announced. "Thank you, ladies. Next pair!" Cammie and Corky jumped in and they, too, passed their test with ease. Soon all the Beaver girls had earned canoe privileges, except for Tina.

"Congratulations to all of you," Roger said. He flashed a grin. "I'll organize a Beaver canoe trip tomorrow morning, and I might even persuade Miss Pepper to pack us a treat." He pointed to a small island toward the middle of the pond. "We'll have a picnic."

Rebecca left the waterfront feeling as buoyant

as if she were still floating. *I passed my swimming test!* she thought proudly.

After she changed, Rebecca headed to Crafts, where she sat by herself. The events of the past days still rankled, from the stolen letter and the slimy frog in her sheets to the stolen role of narrator in *Hiawatha.* As she sewed a design on her dress, she tried to guess who was behind the mean tricks. Corky was always the first to come to mind. She had been jealous when Ginny had chosen Rebecca to be narrator, and again when Rebecca had gotten Mama's letter. But now Corky was the narrator, just as she wished. Cammie had wanted the stamp; she might have taken the envelope, but why would she take the letter, too? That wasn't just a prank—it was stealing.

Rebecca's thoughts kept returning to Tina. She had let Rebecca down more than once. She hadn't stuck up for Rebecca when Corky called for the voting, and she had laughed with the others when Corky called Rebecca a fibber. She was always disappearing at odd moments, too.

Rebecca wanted to believe that Tina was her friend, but could she trust her? Rebecca thought about the girls who had voted with Corky the other day. One of them might have taken the letter just to impress Corky. The one thing Rebecca was sure of was that she hadn't lost the letter accidentally. She had placed it carefully under her pillow. But how would she find the culprit?

A camp song caught Rebecca's ear, and she looked up. Sunny was singing. Her personality matched her nickname—she was always cheerful, Rebecca mused. Still, even Sunny had sided with Corky when the girls had voted for the narrator.

Several campers joined the song, and soon a rousing rendition of "She'll Be Coming 'Round the Mountain" reverberated through the tent. The tune was infectious, and soon Rebecca couldn't help joining in.

As she sang, the knot in her stomach seemed to loosen. *Maybe the frog and the letter were just harmless pranks after all,* she thought. *Or maybe Mama's letter just fell through a crack and down to the floor. I'll look again now that it's daylight.*

Suddenly, one of the younger girls let out a cry, and her sewing scissors clattered to the floor.

"Oh dear, Patty," Babs said, "you've nicked yourself." Patty wailed as Babs wound a clean strip of cotton around her bleeding finger. "Would one of you girls take Patty to the nurse?" she asked.

"I will," Rebecca volunteered. She didn't mind getting away for a while. She tried to cheer Patty up as they left the Craft tent. "Remember what the Loonies say—Nurse Jane, Nurse Jane, she will take away your pain!"

Patty sniffled, holding her finger in the air while Rebecca held her other hand and led her to the medical tent. Nurse Jane cleaned the cut and wrapped a soft bandage around it. She wiped Patty's tears and poured her a glass of lemonade from a pitcher.

"That's going to heal very quickly," Nurse Jane assured the girl. "Stay out of the water, and tomorrow I'll change the bandage and check the cut again." Patty examined her bandaged finger and seemed relieved.

"Oh, Beckie," Nurse Jane said, "would you mind returning this pitcher to Miss Pepper?"

"I can go back to Crafts by myself," Patty offered. "I'm okay now."

As Patty skipped off, Rebecca walked to the dining hall. The door to the kitchen was ajar, and Rebecca saw Miss Pepper step out the back door balancing a tray with a plate of graham crackers and a tall glass of milk. Beyond her, Rebecca could see a camper sitting on a blanket.

"Stay in the sunshine," said the cook, "and eat everything. You've missed too many snacks already." She bent over to set the tray on the blanket and the camper turned. It was Tina!

What was she doing there? And how could Tina have missed a snack? No one else got extra food. Rebecca thought back to the times when Tina had seemed to disappear from the group. This morning, Tina had missed the swim test and Crafts. Now here she was, sunning herself and having a private picnic outside the kitchen!

Rebecca inched closer to the kitchen doorway.

"Sometimes it's hard to get away," Tina was saying.

Miss Pepper patted Tina's shoulder. "I know, but it's important. Now, be sure to drink all your malted milk. I want you as plump as a cherub before summer ends."

Rebecca could barely believe this was the same woman who was usually so snippy. Suddenly she remembered something she'd overheard on the very first day of camp: Mr. Dee had warned Miss Pepper about giving snacks to someone. Had he been referring to Tina? Rebecca frowned, trying to recall what Mr. Dee had said exactly. It was something about the health committee showing up—*"if she's here eating a snack, they're bound to ask questions."* But why would the health committee care about a camper getting extra food?

Miss Pepper turned, and her eyebrows lifted in alarm. "Out of the kitchen!" she ordered sharply. She hurried back inside and slammed the back door closed behind her.

Rebecca felt sure of one thing—she wasn't supposed to have seen Tina resting outside the kitchen with a tray of crackers and milk.

"Nurse Jane asked me to return this pitcher," Rebecca said casually, pretending she hadn't noticed anything unusual. She set the pitcher on the worktable and hurried out.

She walked quickly back to the Crafts tent, turning the scene over and over in her mind. It was probably nothing, really—and yet it was odd—and frankly inexplicable. Why was Tina getting special treatment from Miss Pepper? Yet Rebecca felt pretty sure that if she asked Tina about it, she wouldn't get a clear answer. It seemed that the harder Rebecca tried to become friends with Tina, the less she knew about her.

10
CANOEING AND CONFIDENCES

The next morning a blanket of fog shrouded Camp Nokomis, but that couldn't spoil Rebecca's excitement over the canoe trip. She hurried to complete her morning chore, clearing the platters from the serving table and stacking them in a pan of sudsy water. Then she headed to the Beaver tent for her toothbrush.

Dottie, Cammie, Josie, and Sunny were playing hand games by the flagpole. They giggled as their hands slapped together in a pattern, faster and faster.

"Did you already finish your chores?" Rebecca asked as she passed them.

Josie answered in the same rhythm as the hand game, never missing a beat. "Mine—is—almost—done!"

Rebecca wondered why Josie was standing around playing games if she hadn't completed her chore. She pulled her toothbrush from her carpetbag and headed to the washbasin, annoyed to find that there was no water. Suddenly, Corky scurried over, set a large bucket of fresh water beside the basin, and then scooted off to the Beaver tent without a word.

As Rebecca brushed her teeth, Dottie approached. "Listen, Beckie," she murmured, "I'm really sorry about the vote the other day. I didn't want to do it."

"Then why did you?" Rebecca asked.

"I . . . I . . . *had* to," Dottie said. "Otherwise, someone said we might find frogs in our beds—or snakes!"

"You know who put the frog in my bed?" Rebecca demanded.

Dottie's face turned pink. "Well, not *exactly.*" Rebecca waited for her to say more, but Dottie just fidgeted with her bow, twisting it between her fingers.

"Fine, then don't tell me! I'm not going to

let this spoil my day again." Rebecca turned abruptly and headed back to the tent. The flaps were tied open and Rebecca saw Corky inside, sweeping the floor. Rebecca frowned. Why was Corky doing so many chores? While Rebecca had been clearing the breakfast platters, Corky had been filling the wood bucket for the stove, and just a few minutes ago, she had brought fresh water for the basin.

A wave of understanding swept over Rebecca. No wonder Corky had been late to flag-raising the past few days. She must have promised to do chores for the girls who voted for her to be narrator! And if they didn't agree right away, she had probably threatened them with nasty pranks. Instead of earning their votes, she had bought them with bribes and threats.

*I'd rather be alone all week than **force** someone to be my friend,* Rebecca thought.

Corky raced to the clearing just as the flag reached the top of the pole. Rebecca eyed her warily. It seemed that Corky would do anything to get what she wanted.

The girls sang "America the Beautiful," a song Rebecca had just learned at camp. She had grown to love starting each day with it. The Loonies had changed one of the words from "brotherhood" to "camperhood." When they got to that line, the girls joined hands, swaying to the music. Rebecca held hands with the girls standing on either side of her, but it only made her feel lonelier. Why didn't she have a single friend who would stand up against Corky's bullying? The other Beaver girls had wanted Rebecca to be the narrator—she hadn't begged them for the part.

Rebecca lagged behind as Ginny led the Beaver girls down to the canoes, carrying a knapsack filled with food. The air was heavy with humidity, and wisps of mist floated across the pond like tiny ghosts chasing each other.

"I think the fog is lifting," Roger said, "but we'll stay close together. I don't want a windigo to carry you off for a snack." Several of the girls stared at Roger, and Ginny eyed him critically. "I'm joking!" he said with a wide grin.

He placed the bulging knapsack into one of the canoes. "We'll stop at the island for a break and a small feast, courtesy of Miss Pepper. Now choose a paddling partner." He turned to Ginny. "You'll be in my canoe."

Ginny stepped back. "I was planning to help Babs in Crafts," she protested, but Roger nudged her toward a canoe.

"Babs will do just fine without you," he said, "and I need an extra chaperone with all these campers." Ginny stepped into the front of a canoe without another word of protest.

Tina took Rebecca's hand. "Let's be partners," she said, and Rebecca felt her mood lifting along with the fog. Just when she had thought Tina wasn't her friend, she had picked Rebecca for her partner. Suddenly she thought of something. "You didn't take the swim test!" Rebecca said.

"I already passed," Tina replied as Roger eased her into the back of a sleek yellow canoe.

"You're the guide," he said, handing Tina a paddle. Rebecca settled in the front and picked up a paddle lying at her feet. "You're the lookout," Roger told her. *I'll watch out for windigos*, Rebecca thought, peering through the mist with a slight shiver as Roger pushed the canoe into deeper water.

Tina's strong strokes propelled the canoe forward, and Rebecca heard all the paddles slapping and splashing against the water. Roger and Ginny skimmed expertly between the girls and gave them tips on holding their paddles.

When they reached the island, Roger helped Ginny step out onto dry land and then pulled the other canoes onto the sand.

While Roger and Ginny spread out a large blanket and unpacked the food, the girls began to explore. Rebecca saw that Tina was picking a thick bouquet of daisies.

"I'm going to make flower chains with these," said Tina.

Rebecca sat beside her on the stubby grass and watched as she deftly looped the flowers into a chain. "Can I try making one?" Rebecca asked.

"Sure, it's simple," Tina said, and she showed Rebecca how to split the stems and link the flowers. Rebecca felt a warm bond with her bunk mate as they worked together. By the time the rest of the Beavers had returned from their tramp, Rebecca and Tina had each fashioned flower garlands for their hair.

"I crown you Princess Morning Sun," Tina said with a laugh.

"And I crown you Princess Strawberry Moon," Rebecca replied.

"Can lowly mortals join you?" Corky asked, reaching for a handful of oatmeal cookies. "I didn't know that we were in the company of royalty."

"I can make these for everyone," Tina offered, reaching for an apple.

"Oh, that would be nifty," Josie said. "We can wear them back to camp." She reached over and nicked Corky's cookies. "I think these are mine," she said.

"Hey! Give those back," Corky demanded.

Josie started munching a cookie. "But you *owe* me—remember?"

"Pipe down!" Corky said in a raspy whisper.

"I remember." She walked off with a pout.

More bribes, Rebecca thought to herself. The girls polished off the cookies and fruit and folded the blanket back into the empty knapsack. Soon they were paddling back to camp.

The mist had burned off, and in spite of lingering clouds there was a clearer view across the water. The camp dock looked far away, and Rebecca's arms ached. She rested the paddle across her lap while Tina kept the canoe on course.

"You're awfully good at paddling," Rebecca said over her shoulder. "I'm completely tired out."

"After I hurt my leg, I had to use crutches. That really built up my arm muscles," Tina said to Rebecca's back. "I could paddle all day long."

Rebecca caught her breath. It was the first personal thing Tina had shared. Rebecca never had imagined that Tina's leg injury had been serious enough for crutches.

Rebecca started paddling again. "I'm glad you don't need crutches anymore."

"I've gotten much stronger since I came to camp," Tina said.

But we've been at camp less than a week, Rebecca thought. "What happened to your leg?" she asked.

There was a long moment of silence from the back of the canoe before Tina said softly, "I'm sorry, Beckie. I just can't tell you."

"You'd tell me if we were really friends," Rebecca blurted out as the canoe bumped onto shore beside the swimming dock.

Before she could say more, Roger helped them from the canoe. "Good job, Beavers," he praised the girls. He looked up at the dark clouds. "I'll see you this afternoon for a swimming lesson if the weather holds."

After lunch, Rebecca was surprised to receive another letter. She didn't recognize the handwriting on the envelope. Quickly, she slipped it into her pocket. While her tent mates settled in to play checkers or read, Rebecca walked past the privy and along a trail dusted with pine needles. When she was far enough to be out of sight, she sat on a tree stump and opened her letter. It was from Rose. How she missed her friend! Bold, wise Rose would have stood up to Corky. Eagerly Rebecca read her letter:

Dear Beckie,

I'm glad you made it to camp. You can tell me all about it when you get home.

It's rather dull here. The highlight of our day is when a charity group delivers a parcel of food to the doorstep, along with a newspaper. One day there was a bag of penny candies inside, and Mama let us eat our fill.

Papa tries to hide the paper so we won't read how quickly polio is spreading, but I've seen the headlines. Perfectly healthy children get a fever one night, and the next morning they are paralyzed—or dead! The city is in a complete panic.

Even if I could go out, it seems that all the

fun things are off-limits, so be glad you're in the country. Playgrounds are closed. Kids can't take books from the library. And the movie theater won't allow anyone younger than fourteen to buy a ticket.

Mama says the boy in our building who had polio is getting metal braces to support his legs. The doctor thinks that eventually he might walk again with braces and crutches. We are thankful that he survived and hope the quarantine will be lifted soon.

I sure do miss you. Wouldn't we have had fun at camp? Maybe when you get home, the polio scare will be over and we can play hopscotch or feed the pigeons. I send you a very big hug.

The letter had a large circle that Rebecca thought must be the hug, and then Rose had signed her name right in the middle. Rebecca wrapped her arms around herself, trying to feel Rose's warm hug.

11
A SUDDEN STORM

The storm clouds that had hovered over Camp Nokomis on Friday afternoon burst into a tempest of wind and rain overnight. The Beaver girls fastened the tent flaps to keep them from flying open. Brilliant flashes of lightning illuminated the rows of bunk beds for brief seconds, casting shifting shadows on the canvas walls before plunging the girls into darkness. Rebecca wasn't the only camper who lay awake as thunder shook the air and tree limbs creaked and groaned.

In the morning, Ginny carried in some heavy tarpaulins, and the girls sheltered under them as they darted to the dining hall. Mr. Dee lit a fire in the huge stone fireplace and the girls clustered around it, eating oatmeal and drinking hot chocolate. The fire took the chill from the damp air, and its glow cheered the girls. Outdoor activities were canceled, so the campers organized a checkers tournament. The older girls secretly made sure that the Turtles won. Then all the campers scurried back to their tents through the rain to make final preparations for the *Hiawatha* performance.

Babs ducked into the tent, cradling a box under her arm. "I thought you might need to add to your costumes," she said, setting the box on the floor in the center of the tent. "Who's playing a rabbit?"

"I am," Dottie said. She hopped around holding her hands in front of her chest like paws.

"Then this is for you," Babs said. She pulled a mask from the box. Round eyeholes were cut from an oval piece of birch bark, and a pink felt nose was glued on, along with two big white paper teeth. Yarn strings dangled from each side of the mask to hold it in place.

"It even has whiskers!" Dottie exclaimed. She lightly touched a spray of prickly straw sticking out on either side. She hugged Babs, and the Crafts director beamed. Babs handed out the remaining masks—beavers with buck teeth, birds with protruding beaks, and an elongated deer face with twig antlers. The girls couldn't wait to rehearse. They tied on the masks and peered through the eyeholes, giggling with excitement.

"I'm off to work on props!" Babs said and ran back out into the pelting rain.

The other girls were in high spirits as they practiced, and Rebecca wished she could share their enthusiasm. But with every line that Corky read, Rebecca felt more and more dismayed. The narrator should make the poem come alive, not drone on with stops and starts. Rebecca was glad when the rehearsal ended, the costumes were laid aside, and they darted to the dining hall for lunch.

"I know you've been cooped up today," Ginny said as the tables were cleared, "but you'll have to amuse yourselves in the tent this afternoon." She passed out decks of cards and boxed jigsaw puzzles. A few girls had books to read. Ginny added, "If anyone needs me, I'll be in the Crafts tent helping Babs get everything ready for the performance. I can't believe this camp session is almost over. I'm going to miss you all." Then her face brightened. "But we still have tomorrow—and *Hiawatha*—to look forward to!" She headed to Crafts while the Beavers went back to their tent.

"I heard we're having marshmallow sandwiches tonight!" Corky announced.

"Marshmallow *what?*" Josie asked.

Corky was pleased to explain. "We did that last year," she began. "First, you toast a marshmallow over the fire until it's hot and gooey. Then you plop it onto a graham cracker, lay on a square of chocolate, and top it with another cracker. It's the sweetest treat you'll ever eat!"

"You rhymed!" Sunny laughed.

"That sounds like fun," said Josie, "but what are we going to do now? I'm really bored."

"We could sing," Sunny suggested.

"Or play a parlor game," Cammie said.

"I've got it!" Corky said. "Let's have a scavenger hunt!"

"In this rain?" Bertie asked. "I'm not going out again unless it's for marshmallow sandwiches."

"We'll have it right in the tent," Corky said.

"How can we go on a hunt inside the tent?" Dottie asked. "We know everything in the whole place."

"Not everything," Corky said, and Rebecca saw a mischievous gleam in her eyes. Corky rubbed her chin and appeared to be thinking, but Rebecca had the uneasy feeling that Corky had a plan all hatched out. Was she going to spring another trick on Rebecca?

"I've got it," Corky said at last. "We'll each come up with an item and see who can find it."

Rain pounded the tent, and the gloomy day seemed to grow darker and colder. Rebecca sat on the edge of Tina's bed and pulled her sweater tighter.

"Here's one," Sunny said. "Who can find a pinecone?"

"That's too easy," said Bertie, jumping down from her bunk and rummaging in her carpet-bag. "I've been collecting little ones to take home. They'll make nifty Christmas decorations next winter." She pulled out a handful of small pinecones.

"Here's a harder one," Cammie said. "Who can find something from a creature of the woods?"

"Do birds count?" Josie asked.

Cammie nodded. "Sure, they live in the woods."

Josie slid a burlap packet from under her mattress. She carefully unfolded it and revealed a collection of feathers. "I've been collecting these," she said. "You don't find bird feathers in the city—unless they're from pigeons." The girls marveled over the collection, especially the bright blue jay feathers with dots of white. Josie folded the burlap around the delicate treasures and set them aside.

"My turn," Corky said brightly. "Who can find something we've never seen before?"

"I found a mussel shell at the edge of the pond," Dottie said.

"Pooh," Corky said dismissively. "I've seen those."

"How about our headbands?" Cammie asked. "We just finished them."

Corky shook her head. "We've all seen headbands. We need to scavenge for something completely new."

"But it has to be inside the tent," Josie reminded her.

"Right," Corky agreed. She spun around slowly, pointing to the corners of the tent and up at the pitched roof. Rebecca's body tensed. Suddenly, Corky shook her finger as if it had landed on the perfect thing. "There!" she cried, pointing at Tina's trunk.

The color drained from Tina's face. "Stay out of my things," she said hoarsely.

Corky seemed to waver, but her hesitation lasted only a moment. "But, Teeny, we have to find something we've never seen before," Corky said patiently, as if she were talking to a child who didn't understand. "What do you say, Beavers?" she asked.

Rebecca remembered the morning she had almost lifted the trunk lid herself. *I wasn't really going to open it,* she told herself, but she felt a nagging sense of guilt. It would have been wrong to snoop through Tina's trunk when her bunk mate wasn't around. Tina was here now—and she was telling Corky to stay away.

"You'd better leave it alone," Rebecca said, but her voice was tentative. She was itching to know what Tina had in that trunk. Was it possible that Mama's letter was inside? She hoped not.

"It's just a game," Corky said. "We have to find something new!" Swiftly, Corky unknotted the twine, and it dropped to the floor.

Tina rushed forward. "Get away!"

"Teeny must have something really interesting in this big trunk," Corky taunted. "Something mysterious and not so teeny!" Slowly she lifted the creaking lid, letting the suspense build. All the Beavers stared wide-eyed at the trunk. With the lid wide open, Corky reached in and grabbed the bulky canvas bag that Rebecca had seen Tina remove the other morning.

Tina reached out and tried to grab the bag, but Corky swung it out of her reach. As she did, the bag fell open and the contents slid out, crashing to the floor with a rattling clank.

The girls stared at a leather and metal contraption with an array of straps and buckles.

"Heavens to Betsy," said Bertie, "what in the world is it?"

"Is that for riding a horse?" Josie asked meekly.

A look of horror crossed Corky's face. "Saints preserve us—it's a leg brace," she said in a barely audible voice. Lifting her eyes from the brace, she stared at Tina. "You have *polio!*"

12
A GRAVE THREAT

The dreaded word, *polio*, filled the tent with fear like a snake slithering across the floor.

Josie looked horrified. "How could you come here and expose us all?"

"Oh, no," Dottie moaned. "We're going to catch polio!"

Tina's face flushed. "I'm not contagious," she said quietly. She looked down, avoiding the other girls' eyes. "I had it last year, but it's over."

"How could it be over?" Cammie asked. "My mother said it's spreading through the city every day. She thought I'd be safe at camp . . ." Her voice trailed off, and then in a near whisper she added, "What will happen when Mama hears there's polio right here in my tent?"

Tina shook her head. "It's no different from a

cold. You can't catch a cold from someone who had one last year, can you?"

"Why didn't you tell us, then?" Cammie asked.

"Because I knew you'd never understand," Tina responded, as tears welled up in her eyes. "I was afraid that if you found out, you'd never be my friends." She glanced at Rebecca and then lowered her eyes again.

Rebecca blanched. "If you're really not sick anymore, why do you have a brace?" she asked.

Tears spilled down Tina's cheeks. "My leg is still weak," she said in a choked voice, "but I've been getting stronger since I've been at camp. I just need the brace for support sometimes." She strapped the heavy contraption around her leg. As each buckle clanked closed, the girls winced. "See?" said Tina, her leg held stiffly. "It's just to help me walk."

The girls closest to her backed away.

"We've got to tell Mr. Dee," Josie said. "Now."

Tina wiped at her cheeks. "I'll talk to him myself," she said firmly.

Rebecca stepped hesitantly toward her bunk mate, but Tina whirled around. *"Leave me alone,"* she said, her voice cracking. She untied the tent flaps and limped along the muddy path. The rain had stopped, leaving huge wet drops dripping from the tree boughs.

In the uncomfortable silence, the other Beavers looked at one another uncertainly.

"Do you think Mr. Dee will send Tina home?" asked Dottie.

"Maybe we really *can't* catch polio from her," Bertie said. "She must have had a health certificate from her doctor like the rest of us."

Rebecca felt Rose's letter rustle in her pocket. She had written that perfectly healthy kids came down with a fever one night, and by morning they were paralyzed—or dead. Rebecca shuddered. Yet Tina had said you couldn't catch polio from someone who had already recovered from it. Would she lie about something this serious? Rebecca wanted to believe her, but wasn't sure whether she could trust her.

That evening, Tina wasn't at supper, and

neither was Mr. Dee. The Beavers whispered together about their absence.

"Where's Mr. Dee?" Rebecca asked Ginny, trying to sound casual.

"He went to the train station to use the telephone," Ginny replied. "He does that every now and then, when he needs to call the city to talk to the Children's Society." Ginny didn't seem to think anything out of the ordinary was going on.

Rebecca wondered if Mr. Dee was reporting Tina's illness to Miss Henry. What would happen to Tina?

Corky leaned over and whispered in Rebecca's ear, "Sure an' he's sending Teeny home. Saints preserve us, I hope we don't get sick!"

That evening around the campfire, as the other campers exclaimed over their marshmallow sandwiches, nobody seemed to notice that the Beavers were unusually quiet and subdued. Rebecca had looked forward to the campfire treat but was too upset to enjoy it. At last the girls sang "Taps" and then headed to their tents.

A Grave Threat

When Rebecca stepped inside the Beaver tent, she was startled to see Tina in her bunk, the blanket nearly covering her head.

"I thought for sure Mr. Dee had sent her home," Dottie murmured to the others.

Rebecca walked to her bunk with apprehension. She would be sleeping right above Tina once again. *She can't be contagious,* Rebecca reassured herself, *or Mr. Dee would never have let her stay.* Then a frightening thought occured to her. Tina was awfully good at keeping secrets. What if Mr. Dee *didn't know?*

As she pulled herself up onto her bunk, she heard Tina mutter under her breath, "Some friend you turned out to be. You deserve more than a frog in your bed."

Rebecca felt as if she had been stung by an angry bee. Was it Tina who had hidden the frog in her sheets after all? Suddenly Rebecca couldn't hold back the feelings that had been boiling inside her for days. "I tried to be your friend," she blurted out, "and you kept this a secret from me."

Ginny entered the tent, and the girls hurried silently into bed. "You're awfully quiet tonight," Ginny said. "I know camp is nearly over and that's always sad, but we still have the *Hiawatha* performance to look forward to." Settling on her stool, she read several pages. Then she said good night and carried the lantern out, leaving the tent in darkness.

Rebecca thought she heard Tina crying softly in the bunk below, and she felt a tightness in her chest, but she was still hurt by Tina's accusation. She leaned close to the edge of her bed, picking up the argument where it had ended when Ginny had come in. "Friends are supposed to trust each other," she whispered.

"And *you*," Tina wept, "*you* didn't trust me enough."

Rebecca lay awake a long time, listening to the now-familiar night noises: the chirping crickets, the croaking frogs, the Beaver girls whispering to each other, and a new noise she tried to ignore, but could not—the sound of Tina's smothered sobs.

A GRAVE THREAT

Rebecca didn't know what had awakened her. She blinked in the darkness and instantly remembered the awful events of the day before, and Tina's harsh accusation—*some friend you turned out to be.* With a sinking feeling, she realized that Tina had had good reason for not sharing her secret. The incident with the trunk had proved it: the girls in Beaver were all afraid of Tina now, and once the rest of the camp found out about her polio, she would be an outcast.

Rebecca swallowed a lump in her throat. She should have stopped Corky from opening the trunk. If she had, none of this might have happened.

Suddenly, Rebecca couldn't wait another minute to tell her bunk mate that she understood why Tina hadn't shared her secret. If she was lucky, Tina would give her another chance and they could be friends again. She called softly, but there was no reply. Tina was sound asleep. Rebecca slipped down and kneeled next to her bed. "Tina," she whispered. She tried to shake her bunk mate awake and felt the lumpy bedding yield under her fingers. Pulling the blanket back, she saw the canvas sack that had held the brace. It was stuffed with an extra blanket. Tina was gone.

Standing in her nightclothes, Rebecca scanned the tent. Although she had promised Ginny never to go out alone at night, she stepped cautiously outside in her bare feet. She checked the privy first, but it was empty.

Trees sighed in the breeze, and every rustling leaf sounded like a creature on the prowl. Rebecca felt a rising panic. *Where would Tina go?* Silently she crept to the counselors' tent and peered through the open flaps. Nurse Jane and Babs were playing cards by the light of a lantern. They talked quietly while the other counselors slept nearby. If Tina were there, Rebecca would have seen her.

Rebecca wondered if she should awaken

Ginny. How much did Ginny know about Tina? If Ginny found out what had happened in the Beaver tent, it would surely be worse for all of them.

All Rebecca knew for certain was that she had to find Tina. She stared into the dark forest. If Tina had gone into the woods, she could be in real danger. Rebecca hurried back into the tent and began to dress. As she did, Corky murmured groggily, "What's going on?"

"Go back to sleep," Rebecca whispered as she ducked out of the tent.

She followed the trail that led to the main building, and listened from the porch. The sound of snoring came from behind Mr. Dee's closed door. Clearly, Tina wasn't there.

Rebecca retraced her steps. Just as she stepped onto the path that led away from camp, she heard a voice behind her.

"What are you up to?" Corky demanded.

Rebecca was surprised to see Corky fully dressed. "I think Tina ran away," she said, adding, "not that you'd care."

Corky tossed her head defiantly. "Don't blame me. How could I know what she was hiding in that trunk?"

Rebecca tried to keep her voice down, but her anger gave it a raspy edge. "You didn't have to know," she retorted. "It wasn't any of your business what was in there. Why didn't you stop when Tina told you to leave it alone?"

"It was a game," Corky sputtered. "Just a harmless game."

"*None* of your games are harmless," Rebecca said. "They're mean."

"Everything I did was just a prank," Corky argued. "No one got hurt."

"Not yet," Rebecca snapped. "But what if Tina does get hurt? What if she's lost in the woods? If anything happens to her, it will be all your fault."

Corky's shoulders slumped, and all her bluster drained away. "I didn't know about the brace, and then . . . it was too late." Corky started to sniffle and wiped her eyes with her sleeve. Why, she was crying!

A Grave Threat

A wave of shame washed over Rebecca. In her heart, she knew Corky wasn't the only one at fault. Rebecca could have stood up for Tina. She should have stopped Corky at the start. But deep down, Rebecca realized, she had wanted to know what was inside the trunk. Her voice softened. "It's my fault, too," she confessed. "That's why I've got to find her."

Corky straightened her shoulders. "I'm coming with you."

Rebecca nodded. In spite of her distrust of Corky, at least she wouldn't have to search alone. She remembered the night she had gone out to wash her face and had heard the eerie hooting in the forest. She'd feel safer with someone else along, even if it was Corky.

The girls picked their way past the main building, studying the intersecting paths that wound through the woods.

"She can't travel very fast with her weak leg," Corky said. "And how could she find her way in the dark? I can barely see my own feet."

The girls approached a fork in the trail and

looked in both directions. The clouds that had covered the moon drifted apart, and in the pale light Rebecca saw footprints in the soft mud. She bent down and examined them.

"Look," she said, "the right foot made a deep sneaker print, but there's none on the left side." She studied the ground more closely. "Here's something odd. There's a round dent in the mud on each side." Rebecca tried to imagine what could have made the perfect circles in the wet ground. Then her mind flashed back to something she had seen in the kitchen. "One morning when I was looking for the wood bucket," Rebecca said, "I peeked into the pantry and saw an old pair of crutches leaning against the wall. They must have been Tina's!"

"If she planned to walk a long way, maybe she needed the crutches for extra support," Corky said.

Rebecca nodded, remembering Tina's difficulty on the hike. She scanned the tracks. "Come on. Tina must have gone this way." As the girls followed the trail, Corky reached for

Rebecca's hand. Rebecca was surprised how comforting Corky's hand felt.

Deeper into the woods, the clouds hid the moon once again. Rebecca's pulse raced. "Do you know where this trail leads?" she asked.

Corky shook her head. "If I ever was here before, I don't recognize it."

Suddenly, Rebecca pulled Corky to a halt and pointed ahead. A faint light blinked in the darkness.

"That's not fireflies," Rebecca said.

"Maybe—maybe it's Tina," Corky said uncertainly.

"But where would she get a lantern?" asked Rebecca. "And Tina's too short to hold it so high in the air." She swallowed hard. "It seems to be floating."

"Do you believe there's a windigo?" Corky blurted out.

Rebecca hesitated. "I'm not sure. I mean, I think maybe Roger made it up." She tried to sound more certain than she really felt.

"What else would be out in the woods this

late?" Corky asked in a trembling voice.

Rebecca had no answer to give her.

Holding hands tightly, the girls followed at a safe distance, trying to see who—or what—held the light. The light veered to the left, and in one brief flash they saw the silhouette of a tall figure. Then it was shrouded in inky darkness.

Arrrroooo! Arrrroooo! Rebecca's skin prickled with fear. This was nothing like the hooting call that she had heard before. The howl pierced the quiet woods and lingered in the air.

Corky wrapped her arms around Rebecca and held on tightly. In a choked voice she cried, "It's the windigo!"

13
INSIDE THE CAVE

Rebecca's heart was pounding so fiercely, she was sure it was echoing like a drumbeat.

"There *is* a monster in the woods!" Corky hissed. "What if it captured Tina?"

Rebecca moved forward cautiously and saw more of the strange prints embedded in the dirt. "Tina passed this way," she announced. "If the windigo had grabbed her, she wouldn't be leaving prints." She didn't tell Corky that in addition to Tina's one-legged footprints, a second set of much larger prints was right alongside.

The girls pushed on, watchful of everything around them. The only sounds were branches creaking in the rising wind. Still, the windigo call had been so close and so chilling. The two girls held hands without talking.

143

The path rounded a sharp bend, and the girls stumbled onto a dark mass of boulders. It looked strangely familiar, but Rebecca couldn't think why. Suddenly she remembered. "This might be the place I found when we were lost in the woods," she told Corky.

Corky's eyes were round with fear. "D'you remember the story Roger told us about the windigo that took the shape of a heap of boulders?" she breathed.

Rebecca nodded. She could almost hear Roger's voice telling of the two sisters who came upon the mysterious rocks, and how a fearful monster rose up from the boulders. Her eyes followed the path as it wound around the rocks and then disappeared in the darkness.

A gust of wind whipped through the trees and threw branches across their path, and a low *whoooshh* wafted through the air.

The girls raced for the shelter of a tree trunk and stood like statues, afraid to twitch an eyebrow. Rebecca feared that their panting breath was loud enough to give them away. "That's the sound we heard when we got lost on the hike," she said. "We must be near the cave."

"Let's get back to camp," Corky whimpered, "before the windigo catches us."

Rebecca's head felt light. She longed for the safety of the tent, but what if Tina needed help? She tried to hide her fear as the trees lashed in the wind and the strange sound—almost a moan—grew louder and then died away.

"I'm going ahead," Rebecca declared. She willed herself to move forward, and Corky followed reluctantly, crouching behind Rebecca's back.

The girls began clambering over the low boulders, their feet slipping against patches of damp moss. They stopped atop a flat rock, and Corky gripped Rebecca's arm. "There's another light," she whispered, pointing to a faint orange glow flickering at the mouth of a cave. "Sure an' it's the windigo cave I heard about last summer. Please, Beckie, *please*," Corky wailed. "Let's get away from here!"

"But what if Tina's hurt—or captured?"

"If it's the windigo that has her," said Corky, a note of fear rattling her voice, "then we'll be captured too."

Wisps of smoke wafted from the cave opening, carried on the wind. Rebecca tried to steady her voice. "You can go back if you want, but I'm going in. Someone built a fire in there, and it might be Tina."

"Or whoever *captured* Tina," Corky said. She seemed rooted to the rock. "What if it's the windigo?"

"Do you think a windigo would build a fire?" Rebecca asked, creeping toward the cave.

"Well, they do eat children—maybe they cook them first, over a fire," said Corky as the girls hesitated outside the cave entrance.

Whoooshh! Again the eerie sound filled the air. Corky cowered behind Rebecca, her breath coming in ragged gasps. Then she bent down and picked up a sharp stone. "For protection," she whispered.

With halting steps, the two girls crept through a tunnel toward a glimmering light.

Rounding a turn at the end of the passageway, Rebecca squinted into a rocky hollow as large as a room. Behind a flickering fire, huge shadows played like black specters across the cave wall. Rebecca pulled back and flattened herself against the rough tunnel.

Over the crackling of the fire, a deep voice chanted,

> *Does not all the blood within me*
> *Leap to meet thee, leap to meet thee,*
> *As the springs to meet the sunshine,*
> *In the Moon when nights are brightest?*

"Blood," Corky gasped, her face ashen in the dim light. "I heard him say *blood!*"

There was a brief pause, and then a higher voice responded,

> *Onaway! My heart sings to thee,*
> *Sings with joy when thou art near me,*
> *As the sighing, singing branches,*
> *In the pleasant Moon of Strawberries.*

Rebecca blinked. *Moon of Strawberries?* She fought a hysterical urge to laugh—though she couldn't tell if it was from relief or terror. "Corky!" she rasped. "It's *Hiawatha!*" The chanting voices echoed hollowly off the rocky walls, yet they sounded strangely familiar. Rebecca peered into the cave again. Beneath the huge black shadows looming against the cave wall, two small, hunched figures were visible in the orange firelight. Suddenly one of them rose up. Startled, Rebecca lurched backward, bumping into Corky. The stone fell from Corky's hand and clattered on the loose rocks underfoot.

"Who's there?" bellowed a husky voice.

Corky gave a strangled cry and crumpled to the rocky ground like a rag doll.

"Oh, don't faint," Rebecca pleaded, trying to pull Corky up. "We've got to get out of here!"

Behind her, Rebecca heard footsteps. She looked back into the cave, quaking with fear at what she might see. But instead of a fearsome monster, two human faces stared at her through the dim light. Rebecca's eyes widened with surprise as Ginny and Roger stared back at her.

"What are you girls doing out here?" Roger asked. "Why aren't you in bed?"

Rebecca's voice was raspy. "We're trying to find Tina. She's disappeared!"

Corky staggered to her feet, her shoulders shaking as she sobbed. "We thought the windigo caught her. We've heard terrible howls in the woods and hissing coming from the cave." Rebecca could barely believe this was the same bossy girl who had been so full of bluster.

"Now, now," said Roger awkwardly. "Surely you girls don't really believe that monster myth? I just wanted to give you a bit of a fun scare."

Ginny patted Corky's back, trying to calm her. "The cave sound *is* eerie, but it's only the wind blowing through the passages," Ginny said. "There's a small opening in the cave roof, and when the wind gusts just right, it makes that odd sound." She put her arm around Corky. "It's just a trick of Mother Nature."

Corky's sobs turned to hiccups, and she regained some of her feistiness. "Why, imagine the likes of you two," she sniffed, "sitting in a cave reading romantic verses in the firelight—I suppose *that's* Mother Nature at work, too?"

Rebecca thought she saw Ginny and Roger exchange embarrassed glances. But relieved though she was at Ginny's explanation of the whooshing sound, it didn't explain where Tina was.

"Windigo or not, Tina could still be in danger," said Rebecca. "We think she's run away."

Roger rubbed his forehead thoughtfully. "I have an idea where she might be. You two get back to camp with Ginny."

"Not without Tina," Corky declared.

Roger considered this. "All right, we'll go together. It's not far."

What's not far? Rebecca wondered as Roger doused the fire and led the way out of the cave.

14
TINA'S SECRET

Roger climbed nimbly over the rocks, giving Ginny and the girls a hand. Then he took out a small gadget and flicked it on, casting a pale, blinking beam of light on the path.

"Whatever is that thing?" asked Corky. "It's not a lantern—it's like magic!"

"It's called a flashlight," Roger explained, showing her how he could switch it off and on. "Nifty, isn't it?"

Rebecca and Corky exchanged a knowing look—*that* was the light that had frightened them earlier. Instead of a windigo, it was Roger lighting the path to the cave.

Rebecca felt the events of the night crowding in on her. She was almost too exhausted to put one foot in front of the other, but her concern for

Tina kept her going. Corky linked her arm into Rebecca's as they left the cave and walked back into the gloomy forest.

The trees stood like towering sentinels guarding a secret. Thorny branches scratched at Rebecca's legs as she followed Roger and Ginny along a narrow path nearly hidden in the undergrowth. At last, they stepped into a clearing, and Rebecca saw a farmhouse nestled at the edge. A yellow light shone through one window.

Roger led them to the door and knocked insistently. After a few moments it opened a crack, and Rebecca was startled to see Miss Pepper standing in a bathrobe and slippers.

"Is she here?" Roger asked, and the cook nodded. She opened the door wide, and they all stepped inside.

"I don't understand," Rebecca said. "Why would Tina come here?"

"Where else would she go?" Miss Pepper asked. "Because of the way you girls treated her, she struggled all the way home in the dark."

"Home?" Corky repeated. "But I thought you said she was *here*."

Miss Pepper turned down a hallway, motioning the girls to follow. She ushered them into a small, sparsely furnished room. A calico quilt covered a narrow bed. A pair of crutches leaned forlornly against the faded blue wall. Tina's brace had been dropped on the floor beside them.

Tina lay curled under the quilt but quickly sat up when the girls entered. "What are you doing here?" she demanded. "Just leave me alone!"

"We searched everywhere for you," Rebecca said. "I was so worried. We're sorry for what happened." She hung her head as tears spilled over. "*I'm* sorry. Can you forgive me?"

"I never meant for things to end up this way," Corky put in. "Come back to camp."

Tina shook her head. "I should have known that sooner or later you'd all find out about me, and everything would be ruined." Tears rolled down her cheeks. "I should never have tried to be a camper."

153

"But why are you here with Miss Pepper?" asked Rebecca.

Tina wiped her tear-stained cheeks with her sleeve. "Because this is my house." She nodded toward the cook. "She's not Miss Pepper. She's Mrs. Pfeffer—and she's my mother."

Rebecca's eyes widened. "Your mother? But you don't even have the same last name—"

"Sure we do," Miss Pepper interrupted. "*Pfeffer* is a German name that means 'pepper.' That's how I got my nickname."

"Mr. Dee really wanted Miss Pepper for our cook," explained Ginny, "but she could only take the job if Tina could be at camp, too."

Roger added, "At first Mr. Dee said he couldn't allow it, but then he realized that being at camp might help Tina strengthen her weak leg."

"But what about her . . . polio?" Corky asked nervously.

"Once she recovered, no one could catch it from her," Miss Pepper said. She sat down on the bed and put her arms around her daughter.

"Christina is one of the lucky ones. First, because she's alive—and second because the only lasting effect is one weak leg."

Rebecca took a shaky breath, imagining how frightening it would be to have such an illness. Tina was one of the lucky ones, indeed.

"The doctor said I'd just have to learn to live with it," Tina recalled. "But Mr. Dee thought that regular exercise like swimming could help me build up my muscles and walk without crutches—and maybe even without my brace."

"At camp, Tina got stronger every day," said Roger. "I started giving her swimming lessons two weeks ago when the staff arrived to set up. Tina took to the water like a tadpole."

Tina's mouth turned up in a faint smile. "Just before the campers arrived, I stopped using my crutches and started walking without the brace."

"Mornings are the most difficult for her," Miss Pepper said. "She put on the brace when I woke her up to play 'Reveille' each morning, but after a few hours, she could manage without it."

Rebecca remembered the clinking sound of

the brace the morning she had seen Tina take it from the trunk. So that's why Tina's jumper and bloomers were so long, Rebecca realized—to cover the leg brace. And that's why Miss Pepper had been giving Tina extra snacks—she was trying to help Tina get stronger.

"Don't you see?" Tina pleaded. "If I stay at camp all summer, I might not have to use the brace at all. Then I could go back to school—and maybe have friends again." She shook her head. "I should have known it wouldn't work."

"But if no one can catch polio from you now, why can't you go to school?" Corky asked.

"Fear," declared Miss Pepper. "No matter how much we tried to explain, even Tina's best friends wouldn't go near her. Their parents made sure of that, scaring them all to death."

"The teacher put my desk off in a corner, as if even she didn't want me in the class. I finally stopped going to school, and no one asked me to come back."

Now Rebecca understood why Tina wouldn't talk about her limp. She was afraid she'd be hounded out of camp, just as she had been shunned at school. And that was exactly what almost happened. "So that's why you kept all this a secret," Rebecca murmured.

Tina nodded, her eyes downcast.

Ginny spoke up. "I feel partly to blame. I agreed to keep the polio a secret, but now I think it might have been better to be forthright about everything from the start."

Tina looked up at her. "But if the City Children's Society had found out about me, they wouldn't have let me stay. Since I don't live in the city, I was never on their list." She paused. "Mr. Dee broke the rules by letting me be a camper—but he was just trying to help."

"Of course he was," Miss Pepper said briskly. "Now, let's not stand around here." They filed into the kitchen, where Miss Pepper set out a pitcher of cold milk and a heaping plateful of oatmeal cookies.

In the cozy kitchen, Corky recovered her spunk. "Mercy! You should have told us about your leg sooner, instead of acting so suspicious."

"I wasn't acting suspicious," Tina protested.

"Humph!" Corky snorted. "Ain't you the one—"

Ginny corrected her automatically. *"Aren't you the one."*

Corky let out an impatient sigh. *"Aren't* you the one always disappearing like a leprechaun? Changing out of sight, gone from the tent before we wake up, and off to who knows where half the time?"

"Come back with us," Rebecca urged. "We'll explain everything and make sure the other girls understand."

"Tina can't possibly walk back to camp tonight," said Miss Pepper. "She's staying right here at home. After she gets a good night's rest, we'll see."

15
A FLICKERING WISH

Rebecca awoke to bright sunlight streaming through the tent flaps. The Beaver girls were just beginning to stir.

"What time is it?" Josie asked, stretching her arms lazily. "I didn't hear the bugle."

"That's because our bugler ran away," Corky announced. The other girls stared in disbelief as Corky went on. "Rebecca and I were afraid she'd been captured by the windigo!" She let the girls wait breathlessly before telling them more.

Rebecca listened as Corky told the others about their nighttime escapade. She noticed Corky was delighted to have a rapt audience.

"We came to a pile of boulders, just like in Roger's story," Corky said, her green eyes dancing. "And the most horrifying hissing you ever heard was coming out of the cave, which was glowing with smoke and flame. Sure an' we thought Tina was being cooked alive! But I— well, Beckie and I—climbed over the rocks and walked right into the mouth of the cave. We were ready to face whatever was in there, to save poor Tina from a fate worse than death!"

Dottie wrung her hands together. "You found the hissing cave? I've never been so scared as I was when we heard it on the hike."

"Ginny says the eerie sounds were just the wind blowing through openings in the cave," Rebecca put in, but nobody seemed to pay much attention.

"I can't believe we slept through it all!" said Sunny. "Let's plan a hike out there. Wouldn't it be tip-top to crawl through a cave?"

"Not if you thought there was a windigo inside, roasting Tina for dinner," said Corky. "I tell you, it's lurking out there, no matter what Roger says!" Rebecca noticed that Corky was finally calling Tina by her proper name, instead of "Teeny."

"Gosh, you were brave," Josie said, and Corky swelled with pride.

Rebecca remembered how Corky had cowered behind her on the rocks and nearly swooned with fright inside the cave. She smiled to herself. It didn't matter how the story was told. But when Corky reached the part about Miss Pepper's house, she faltered, and Rebecca told the rest—about how Tina had come to Camp Nokomis to regain her strength, and how Mr. Dee had broken the rules to help her, and how Tina had cried because she had no friends at school or at camp.

"*We're* her friends," Bertie said staunchly.

"Of course we are," Cammie agreed.

"I told her to come on back to camp last night, but her ma wouldn't let her," said Corky. "Let's go tell Miss Pepper we want her back." The other girls nodded eagerly at this plan. Then Corky's eyes narrowed shrewdly. "Meanwhile, Ginny and Roger have a bit of explaining to do."

"Oh, but it's so romantic," sighed Sunny, pressing her hands over her heart. "Just imagine reading poetry by the firelight in a secluded cave!"

"I wonder what Mr. Dee will have to say about *that*," Corky retorted. "Looks like our Tina wasn't the only one keeping secrets."

Since they were late, the girls skipped their morning swim. They dressed quickly and headed straight to the dining hall for breakfast.

"Hello, sleepyheads," Ginny said with a bright smile as the girls took their places around the Beaver table. Beside Ginny sat Tina, looking tired and pale. The other Beavers slid quietly into their seats, suddenly tongue-tied.

Rebecca recalled Miss Pepper saying that mornings were the hardest part of the day. She jumped up. "You just sit here," she said to Tina, "and I'll fetch you some pancakes and eggs."

Corky grabbed a pitcher and started pouring milk in Tina's cup.

"Don't start waiting on me," Tina protested. "I may be slow, but I can walk around on my own, you know."

"Don't worry," Bertie said, passing Tina a

buttered roll. "This special treatment isn't going to last past breakfast!" She smiled. "It's our way of saying we're sorry."

Roger sauntered over to the Beaver table and leaned over Ginny's chair. "I see all the Beavers are together—where they belong," he said with a jaunty grin.

Rebecca pinned him with a sharp stare. "Roger, when Corky and I were in the woods searching for Tina last night, we heard the strangest sound—a creepy howl that fairly pierced the air! We were sure it was the windigo. What do you think it could have been?"

Roger straightened up and cleared his throat. *"Arrrrrooooo!"*

"Sure an' it wasn't a hoot owl," said Corky. "It was a lovebird!"

Ginny blushed and the Beavers broke into laughter, but their hilarity was stopped by the sudden sound of hard shoes striking the floor. The girls turned to see Miss Henry striding into the building, fanning her face in the heat.

Mr. Dee stood up, dabbing his mouth with a

napkin. "Please continue with your breakfast, girls," he said calmly. He turned to Miss Henry. "As I reported to you on the phone last evening, all the girls are perfectly healthy. One simply has a weak leg from an old bout with polio."

"And why didn't I have that health certificate, Mr. DeAngelis?" asked Miss Henry.

Tina stood up. "He was trying to help me, Miss," she said in a small voice. Pushing back her chair, she limped over to Mr. Dee. "I didn't mean to cause so much trouble. I'll go home right after breakfast."

"You'll do nothing of the kind," Mr. Dee declared. The director's glasses slid down his nose as he turned back to Miss Henry. "I only meant to give Christina an opportunity to benefit from camp. I know she isn't from your district, but I didn't think it was too big a transgression. I had planned to ask your permission, Miss Henry, but I never dreamed the city would suddenly experience such a terrible outbreak of polio. Once the epidemic began, I knew how serious it would be if anyone found out. The other parents would have panicked, which might have forced the entire camp to close."

"Well, Mr. DeAngelis, I must say that the Society was quite disturbed to learn we had an unregistered camper," Miss Henry replied, "especially one that raised so many fears."

Mr. Dee pushed his glasses back into place. "I'm afraid my concern for Christina clouded my judgment. But I can't say that I would have done things any differently, for she has benefited greatly from the food and exercise that camp has provided."

Miss Henry's face softened. "Our mission is to help girls grow stronger and have new opportunities they couldn't otherwise enjoy. Christina certainly meets both goals." She thought for a moment and then added, "We did have too many spaces go begging this session."

Mr. Dee nodded. "I'm sure we can reach a satisfactory solution for all concerned." He ushered Miss Henry into his office and closed the door with a *click.*

After supper, the girls donned their costumes and braided one another's hair. Tina and Rebecca walked to the waterfront arm in arm. Now that they were truly friends, Rebecca was sorry she would be heading home the next day.

Corky plopped down next to Rebecca on the bench around the campfire and handed her the Hiawatha book. "If I hadn't bullied the other girls, they never would have voted for me," she admitted. "I thought that was the only way I'd have friends or get to be narrator." She grinned sheepishly. "It worked last year."

Rebecca opened the book. Her mother's letter was tucked inside.

"I'm sorry, Beckie," Corky said. "I shouldn't have been jealous of you—not about the performance, and certainly not because of mail."

"That's all behind us now," Rebecca said. "But there is just one more thing I have to ask: was it you who put the frog in my bed?"

"Horrors, no!" Corky exclaimed. "I wouldn't dream of touching such a slimy thing." Her eyes danced impishly. "Josie was glad to do it for me—although I had to give away two days' worth of desserts in the bargain."

Rebecca had to smile. "So, you traded a treat for a trick." Then she sighed wistfully. "Camp went by too fast."

"Sure an' we need more time to start over again on the right foot," Corky agreed. She nudged Tina and giggled. "Or the left foot!"

The girls fell silent as Roger lit the campfire and Mr. Dee announced the play. In a ringing voice, Rebecca recited the first passage, beating the drum in time to the poem's rhythm as the Beavers performed without a hitch. Each tent presented their passage, and the poem seemed to come alive. At the end, the campers clapped and cheered.

As the applause died away, Rebecca stepped into the circle and faced the campers. In the flickering firelight, she began to tell a tale.

"One summer, in the Moon of Strawberries, the girls of Camp Nokomis heard the eerie cry of the windigo echoing through the forest around their tents. They vowed they would never set foot into the woods at night—and never wander about alone. But once, on the darkest of nights, two campers ventured out into the forest primeval in search of their missing friend." The campers hung on Rebecca's every word, mesmerized by her story. Some of it was true, and some of it was fanciful, but when she finished spinning her tale, everyone gave her a rousing cheer, and Roger stood up and gave a piercing whistle of approval.

As Rebecca settled back down with her friends, Babs handed out the tiny bark canoes that the girls had fashioned. She had affixed a small candle in each. The counselors lit each candle with a thin taper, and the campers set their canoes afloat, where they made a sparkling procession across the pond.

"It's been a tradition at Camp Nokomis for each camper to make a wish as her canoe floats away," Mr. Dee said.

Rebecca gazed out at the candlelight floating on the water. She remembered what Tina had said her mother called fireflies—"little sparkles of love in the night." Each glowing candle flame seemed like the spark of a growing friendship. Rebecca closed her eyes and made a wish.

Then she turned to the Beaver girls around her. "I'm going to miss you all," she told them amidst hugs and a few tears. Tina was the hardest one to bid good-bye. "I hope you can stay at camp for the rest of the summer and meet new girls."

"If you write to me, I'll write to you," Tina promised.

"Before we sing 'Taps' tonight," Mr. Dee said, "I have one more announcement. Miss Henry informed me yesterday that because of the swift spread of polio in New York City, the authorities won't allow any more children to leave for camp. There will be no new campers here for the rest of the summer." The girls buzzed with astonishment.

"However," the director continued, "when the social workers met with your families at home, your parents all gave permission for you to stay at camp for another full week."

There was a brief moment of stunned silence, and then an exuberant cheer rose up. *Hip, hip, hooray!*

The Beaver girls hugged one another, and Corky was the first to hug Rebecca. "You're going to have to tell your windigo story again," she said with a mischievous grin.

Rebecca grinned back. "Next time, I think you should tell it, Corky. After all, it's your story, too."

And as she walked back to the Beaver tent, arm in arm with Corky and Tina, Rebecca had a feeling that her story would become part of the camp lore—a tale that would be shared around the fire at Camp Nokomis for many summers to come.

LOOKING BACK

A PEEK INTO THE PAST

A crowded New York City street in Rebecca's neighborhood

In Rebecca's time, families knew that the countryside was a nicer and healthier place for children in the summer than the crowded, stifling city. If they couldn't afford to pay for summer camp, parents registered their children with charity organizations, hoping that their children might be able to attend camp for free.

The New York City neighborhood where Rebecca lived had charities that helped immigrants and poor families. Some of the charities ran summer camps to provide city children with fresh air, exercise, and nutritious food. They also wanted to encourage children of different backgrounds to become friends.

Summer camps for boys started in the late 1800s. By 1910, there were girls' camps, too. Charities often outfitted the girls with suitable clothing—loose-fitting bloomers, cool middy blouses, and sneakers.

For New York City kids like Rebecca, the journey to camp began at the cavernous Grand Central Terminal. The children were awed by the massive marble staircase and the ceiling mural studded with stars. Like Rebecca, most of them had never been away from home before. At camp,

When it opened in 1913, Grand Central was the largest train station in the world.

everything felt strange, and homesick children sometimes cried themselves to sleep the first night. By the end of their session, they cried because it was time to leave!

A clanging bell or bugle call roused campers from their bunks each morning. After breakfast, chores, and flag-raising, camp days were filled with swimming and boating, hiking and archery, crafts and games, and of course songs and stories around the campfire—much like summer camps today. But there was one big difference:

Campers in bloomers stand beside neatly made beds. Some people thought bloomers were scandalous, but girls liked being able to move freely.

in Rebecca's time, camps had no bathrooms, so the campers used *privies*, or outhouses, and bathed in lakes or ponds!

Many camps had Indian themes. Like the girls at the fictional Camp Nokomis, campers made Indian costumes and presented plays based on Native

American culture. Some camps even hired people from local tribes to teach native crafts and tell campfire stories. Many northeastern tribes had legends of a windigo, a monster that stalked the forest to capture stragglers, just as in Roger's tales.

In the Camp Fire Girls novels, the campers dressed like Indians and learned Indian skills such as canoeing.

In the summer of 1916, when this story takes place, families were particularly desperate to send their children to camp. A frightening illness called polio, or *infantile paralysis*, was spreading through the city. Perfectly healthy children came down with a mild fever and symptoms of a cold; within hours, they grew critically ill. The disease paralyzed their muscles and affected their ability to walk, move their arms, and sometimes even breathe.

When a child contracted polio, the city nailed a quarantine sign on the building. No one could go in or out for several weeks until doctors decided the patient wasn't contagious. Some children were taken to hospital isolation wards.

Doctors knew that a virus caused polio, but not how to treat it or keep it from spreading. Health officials thought it spread through dirty

A sign on a quarantined building

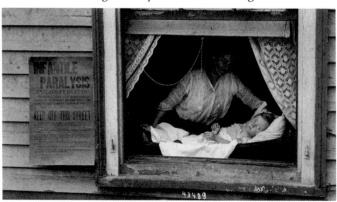

living conditions in poor neighborhoods, perhaps carried by cats, dogs, or flies. They started a cleanup campaign, hosing down the streets and holding fly-swatting contests. But even children in wealthy neighborhoods became ill.

The city tried to stop polio's spread by closing places where children gathered. Fourth of July celebrations were canceled, and children were banned from theaters and libraries. Nearby towns and states refused to let children from New York City cross their borders without health certificates. Some places even hired guards to turn city families away!

That fall, school opening was delayed until cool weather ended the epidemic. Polio had stricken 9,000 children in New York City. About one in four died. Some survivors learned to walk with crutches or braces supporting their legs; others had

A child's leg braces

to use wheelchairs. Although their illness was over, many people were afraid to go near them for fear of infection.

It took years for doctors to discover that a virus in contaminated water caused polio. Finally, in 1954, Dr. Jonas Salk developed a vaccine that prevented people from getting the disease. His pioneering

The most famous polio survivor was President Franklin D. Roosevelt, shown here with a young friend, Ruthie, and his dog, Fala.

work finally eliminated the threat of polio.

ABOUT THE AUTHOR

Jacqueline Dembar Greene is the author of more than thirty fiction and nonfiction books for young readers. The camp setting for *Secrets at Camp Nokomis* was inspired by her research for the American Girl series about Rebecca Rubin. Ms. Greene's previous studies of Native American lore and her interest in ancient caves added to the mystery's plot. She has walked, swum, slid, crawled, and squeezed through caves and caverns throughout North America, Mexico, Puerto Rico, and Europe. She especially loves the random caves scattered around the Hudson Valley of New York, where each one seems to hold its own silent secrets. Ms. Greene lives in Wayland, Massachusetts, with her husband. In addition to writing, she loves to hike, garden, and travel off the beaten path.